I0574195

last chris*t*mas

CHRONICLES
of NICK:
SHADOWS OF FIRE

SHERRILYN KENYON

OLIVER**HEBER**BOOKS

All rights reserved.

No part of this publication may be sold, copied, distributed, reproduced or transmitted in any form or by any means, mechanical or digital, including photocopying and recording or by any information storage and retrieval system without the prior written permission of both the publisher, Oliver Heber Books and the author, Sherrilyn Kenyon, except in the case of brief quotations embodied in critical articles and reviews.

PUBLISHER'S NOTE: This is a work of fiction. Names, characters, places, and incidents either are the product of the author's imagination or are used fictitiously. Any resemblance to actual persons, living or dead, business establishments, events, or locales is entirely coincidental.

Last Christmas Woodward McQueen, LLC ©2023

All rights reserved. No part of this book may be used or reproduced in any matter whatsoever without written permission except in the case of brief quotations embodied in critical articles or reviews.

Cover Design Copyright © Dar Albert Wicked Smart Designs

Printed in the United States of America

Published by Oliver-Heber Books

0 9 8 7 6 5 4 3 2 1

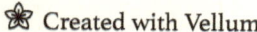 Created with Vellum

1

"We've got them routed, brother. Don't let up!"

Spreading his wings wide, Malphas inclined his head to Itzal. He had no intention of letting any enemy survive this battle. He'd been called one of the deadliest demons in history and reveled in that title.

Indeed, his greatest wish was to become even more feared than the gods.

That was his dream.

His reality...

Malphas was wing deep in guts and swimming in entrails. Covered in blood.

Nirvana!

Nothing made him feel better than this. Than

listening to demons, gods and humans scream out in agony. It was as if a part of his soul was freed every single time they begged him for their lives.

Perhaps that made him sick in the eyes of some.

In his mind, it made him even. None of them had ever cared when he suffered. In fact, most of them had egged the abuse on with a smirk that betrayed their sick sense of satisfaction. Their cruelty had seared his soul until nothing was left other than hatred and bitterness. A need to make them feel the pain of his existence.

Malphas parried a sword stroke from a female Sephirii. Her pale wings glistened against the blood that stained his black ones.

Snarling, he moved to kill her. Until he saw her sword and knew her instantly...

Myone.

Kill her!

He needed to. He must!

And your brother will have no one.

Malphas tightened his grip as he held her wrist in his hand. One stroke. One strike and he'd be able to deliver her head to his father.

Jaden would be furious. He'd probably punish him eternally for daring to take her life. Such an easy thing.

Do it! Do it!

His gaze fell to her flat belly where she grew a child. He could hear its heartbeat.

My nephew. He could sense the boy that innocently lay in ignorance of the bloodshed around them. A boy who would probably pick up a sword to slay both him and his brother who had fathered him.

One stroke would end both mother and child.

And destroy his brother before the child did it for him.

Do it!

That voice would not relent with its demand. Neither would a good demon. A demon would crush them both, without hesitation or mercy.

You are a demon.

He was, but he was something more. The demigod blood in him was at war with the demon. It always had been.

Damn both his halves for never leaving him in peace.

And before he could decide his fate, Myone took advantage of his distraction to plant a short spear in his side. "Die, demon scum!" she snarled in his face as she kicked him back.

That kick caused the tip of the spear to rip across his side, all the way to his back.

Malphas cried out as physical pain tore through him. Even so, he reached for her.

She swung her sword, cutting through his wing. That blow sent him pummeling toward the ground. Malphas tried to change forms, but his pain prevented it. It wouldn't even let him have his natural body.

Cursing, he began peeling off armor as fast as he could. If he didn't lighten his weight, his one good wing wouldn't be enough to save him.

This time it was his own blood that soaked him, making his feathers even heavier. His flight more unsteady.

And the ground was growing nearer. Faster than even his rapid heartbeat. Malphas had never once known fear.

Until now.

The bitter taste burned through his throat as he struggled to slow his speed and save his useless life. Strange how many times he'd bragged that death didn't scare him.

This is a bad way to find out I'm a liar.

Because right then, he wanted to live. Why? He still didn't know. Life had never been kind to him. Not in any way. But here as he was about to leave it, he discovered a ripe vein of desperation that clung to his miserable existence.

And still he fell, reminding him of just how high they'd flown in the battle. So intent on annihilating each other, none of them had paid attention to the fact that the land below was no longer visible.

That the fall alone could kill them, even though they were immortal.

Then, just as he feared nothing could save him, he felt something grab hold of his arm. With a gasp, he looked up and saw his brother.

Itzal grimaced. "Gah! Malphas, how much do you weigh?"

"Be grateful I stripped off my armor."

"I'd be more grateful if you'd diet."

Malphas bit back a laugh as he saw the ground speeding ever closer. Yet not as fast as it'd been a few moments before. Had his brother not interfered, he'd have been a pitiful stain on the scenery by now.

Once they were close to the ground, Itzal dropped him gently on the soft grass. "I'll return when I can. You'd best hide from the humans."

Hide from the humans ... would the degradations never cease? But what choice did he have? He was in too much pain to conceal his demonic form. With his wing damaged, he couldn't fly.

He could fry them, but if he passed out ...

They would have him.

As much as he hated to admit it, Itzal was right. Hide or die.

"Cursed, wretched humans." They should all die. Preferably by his hand, but any means would suit him at the moment.

Groaning, he made his way toward cover. He'd need a place to rest. One where the humans couldn't stumble upon him while he was locked in this form.

Yet as he walked, he realized that his feet weren't the best form of travel. No wonder he preferred flight. This was excruciating and every step seemed to be harder than the last.

"I will not fall." He repeated that litany over and over in his head, determined to walk and be ready to fight.

If only his wounds had ears. Sadly, neither did his legs. They buckled and sent him to the ground.

"I won't die here." Malphas crawled toward the small opening he saw ahead. He only hoped there was no one else in that overhang. Like this, he doubted if he could battle even a mouse.

Malphas moved forward, pushing his sword. The darkness was soothing if not musty. Stale. The stench was such that he could taste it.

At least that was his last thought before the darkness took him.

MALPHAS CAME AWAKE with a sharp jerk. At first, he wasn't sure what had happened. Not until he heard human voices.

"I saw a demon, I tell you. He fell not far from here."

"Then we'll gut him!"

How brave they were when going after a wounded animal. But just like a wounded animal, demons were much more dangerous in this state. A demon's will to survive was far greater than any other species. Indeed, self-preservation was engraved in their DNA.

Never mind the demigod part of him. It would annihilate the world in order to survive.

Forcing himself to rise, Caleb grabbed his sword. *I will not be defeated.* Especially not by a group of *humans*. Petty, smelly, repugnant... he'd never understand why the gods had brought forth such an abomination.

Determined to put them in their graves, he left the quiet cave.

And walked into the middle of what had to be a hundred humans.

Crap.

Worse? He wore nothing on his body other than his orange skin. So much for arrogance. At the moment, he'd be thrilled to have a loincloth.

Thankfully, they were as stunned as he was. Which gave him enough time to rush toward them with a feral scream.

That caused them to wet their breeches as they scattered for the trees. If only they'd stay there. But he was no fool. He had stunned them, and they'd run.

All too soon, they'd come to their senses and realize that even as great a warrior as he was, he was no match for their numbers.

A blast of fire struck the tree beside him. Malphas gasped and looked to see a sorcerer in their mix.

Lovely.

Didn't really change anything, other than his temper. Now, he wanted blood. But first, he needed to get away and find some clothes. As much as he wanted to destroy them, he was aware that he was naked, wounded, and that they seriously outnumbered him.

The mightiest bull can be brought down by a pack of wild dogs.

That was the only lesson his father had ever passed along to his sons. Other than to trust no one. Of course, he hadn't needed his father to teach him the latter given that his mother had schooled him on it first... with the back of her hand.

Clutching his side, he made his way deeper into the

woods. He heard the others calling out to each other, warning them of how dangerous he was.

They had no idea.

Malphas drew a ragged breath and winced as he tried to hide his wings. At first it only spread a wicked pain through his body. But just when he feared he'd pass out from the pain, they returned to his skin.

Trembling from the weight of agony, he moved as silently as possible through the underbrush. Gods, how it galled him to be running from primates.

I'm a Daeve! And a demigod.

He commanded legions.

Sadly, none of those legions were here. Nor did they really care that he was about to get his ass kicked. That was a bit of a problem. And given their loyalty, if they found him like this, they'd be just as likely to kill him as the humans.

Demons were treacherous that way.

Not that anyone could be trusted. He couldn't repeat that litany enough. Everyone betrayed. Everyone lied. In the end, the only one anyone could rely on was themselves.

Except for today. Today, he was betraying himself. His body didn't want to cooperate. It was ready to fall down, and let the humans take him. What difference would it really make? His body might be alive, but he'd died inside a long, long time ago.

Don't you do it! Keep moving!

It took everything he had to move forward.

"He's here!"

Malphas growled as one of the little bastards outed him to his companions. He threw a fireball at the human, then ran as fast as he could in the opposite direction.

They were coming. Faster and in greater numbers.

Malphas ground his teeth, determined to escape them. Blindly, he ran through the trees. Birds scattered to get away from them. Unable to maintain his form through the pain, he felt his body shifting again.

I have to do something...

He went to the wayside and fell, then used his powers to pull leaves and dirt over his body.

"It was right here. I saw it." The humans were just beside him now.

"Could he vanish?" Another man asked.

"He's a demon. He could probably do a lot of things. I imagine vanishing would be right easy enough for one such as he."

"Killing us would be even easier."

Something moved in the brush.

"Get 'em!"

They took off at a dead run away from Malphas's hiding spot.

More relieved than he wanted to admit, Malphas waited for several minutes to ensure they didn't return this way.

Once he was certain that he was safe, he rose slowly.

Thankfully, he was alone. Ominously so.

The only sound was his echoing heartbeat that drummed in his ears. Indeed, even the insects appeared to be silent.

And still the pain ravaged him.

His legs shaking, Malphas renewed his path through the woods, making sure to avoid any places a human might be.

He needed someplace safe to rest. Then he'd be able to return home. Or to battle. Either one was acceptable.

Death was technically a third option. And given the way his body ached, it was a lot more appealing than it'd been earlier.

Indeed, he was almost ready to cut his own throat to escape this agony.

But he wouldn't give his enemies that satisfaction. Not today.

As Malphas broke into a small clearing, he saw a rippling stream. A welcoming sight.

Hesitating, he made sure that no one was near, then

crept toward it. The sparkling water beckoned him in a way he couldn't deny. Until then, he hadn't realized how thirsty he was. But his throat was parched.

Grateful for the small mercy, he fell down beside it and quickly drank his fill.

Malphas let out a relieved breath as he rolled from his stomach onto his side. He spread his black wings wide while he tried to staunch some of the blood leaking from his belly. All he wanted was a few minutes of reprieve.

But a sudden gasp intruded on his peace.

Furious, he rose in one graceful roll and angled his sword with the intent to behead whatever human dared to disturb him.

That was his thought until his gaze locked onto two celestial blue eyes that were filled with fright. The woman's white-blonde hair was pulled back into a long, thick braid, yet defiant strands had come free to curl and tease her pale skin. Her nose was a bit large for her pixie-like face, but it didn't detract from her beauty in the slightest. In fact, that small flaw somehow made her even more beautiful.

And even though she was obviously terrified of him, she bit her lip and approached him very slowly.

Cautiously.

"Are you injured?" In stark contrast to her fragile appearance, her voice was rather deep and sultry.

Seductive.

Stunned that she wasn't screaming or running away, Malphas scowled at her while he debated if he should kill... or kiss her.

"Can you understand me?"

He bared his fangs as she came closer, then hissed, hoping to send her fleeing.

Instead, she froze instantly. "I mean you no harm, demon. I'm a healer." She gestured at his wound. "I can help you, if you let me."

Help him? Was she insane? She was human... they were enemies in this war. She had to know that. His kind had slaughtered hers by the thousands.

Without fail. Without prejudice.

Without hesitation.

And with a glee that was legendary.

Still, she stood there with her arms held out at her sides. No guile. No deception that he could sense. She seemed as sincere as any creature he'd ever known. Not that he'd known all that many who were sincere. The majority of his acquaintances were backbiting bastards who would betray you faster than a heart could beat.

She took a hesitant step forward. "Please... let me

help. If anyone else finds you here, they'll call the others to slay you."

Yes, they would. And he'd kill a lot more of them. They might end him, but they'd pay a steep price for his life.

Malphas narrowed his gaze on her. "Why aren't you calling them to help you?"

"You've done me no harm. You're not threatening me. I don't believe in holding someone accountable for the deeds of others. Only in what he, himself, has done."

And he, himself, had slaughtered hundreds of her ilk. What would she say if she knew the truth?

Swallowing hard, she moved forward again until she reached the tip of his outstretched sword that was still coated in the red blood of his vanquished enemies.

Of the Sephirii warriors who protected the pathetic human horde he hated.

Only when she saw that blood did she hesitate.

He should hate her for her humanity. But she was such a delicate creature of beauty.

What harm could she cause him?

So Malphas lowered the tip of his blade to the ground, and let the sword fall from his hand. He tucked his black wings down by his sides, then hissed as that action caused more pain to slice through his abdomen.

It was so severe that it drove him to his knees and

almost transformed him. Gasping, he tried to rise, but it was useless.

The woman knelt by his side. With the tenderest expression anyone had ever given him, she laid a gentle hand on his cheek. It was the first time in his life anyone had given him such a touch.

One intended to soothe, not hurt.

For a full minute, he couldn't breathe as unknown feelings went through him. More than that, her skin smelled of rose water and honey. A delectable scent that awoke a fierce hunger in his soul.

Yet it wasn't for her blood or bones.

It was something else he craved, and he had no idea what to call it.

"You're burning with fever." She brushed her hand through his hair.

He couldn't believe that she didn't recoil from his unnatural blood red skin tone. Or long orange hair. Rather, she cupped his cheek and stared into his yellow demonic eyes without flinching as she wiped away the black demon's blood on his cheek and lips.

"Can you stand?" she asked gently.

He nodded, not really sure if he could or not.

To his even greater shock, she helped him to his feet. And when her gentle hand brushed against his black wings to help support him, he was lost to her kindness.

"There's a cave where I played as a girl, just over that hill." She jerked her chin to show him the direction. "No one ever goes there. They believe it's haunted. You should be safe to rest within its shelter, and I can tend your wound and bring you food."

"I still don't understand why you would help me."

"Because you need it."

She made it sound so simple. As if his words were foolish.

But he knew people didn't help others. They only preyed.

Amazed by her heart, he shook his head. "Aren't you afraid of me?"

"Petrified."

And she should be. He towered over her frail, fragile human body. It would take nothing to break her into pieces and use her blood and bone marrow to restore his strength and heal his injuries. He'd torn apart men twice the size of her, and they had been trained warriors.

Yet here she stood... unarmed. Defenseless. Her only armor was a thin, light yellow flaxen dress that was so thin, he could see the outline of her body whenever the sun passed through it. She didn't even have on a single piece of jewelry she could stab him with.

Nothing.

Even her nails were trimmed to the quick so that she

couldn't scratch him. She was as harmless as a little mouse.

A part of him wanted to taste her blood to see if it was as sweet as she smelled. That same part of his soul hated her for daring to stand before him like this— for that innocent trust that said she knew he wouldn't hurt her.

It was as if she dared him to prove he was ruthless and uncaring. That he was a demon, through and through. Things he'd vowed to himself he would always be. That he would feel nothing.

Numb to the world and all its pain.

She was his enemy. The very thing his father sought to protect. Malphas had sworn his sword and army to the utter destruction of every member of her pathetic race. To see them put down like the infectious disease they were.

Humanity...

The very word was bitter on his tongue.

Yet as he looked down at her and felt the heat of her hand on his skin...

This wasn't hatred inside him. He wanted to comfort her and chase away the frightened light in her eyes.

"I won't hurt you, little one." He wasn't sure who was more stunned when those words came out of his mouth.

For the first time, the terror faded from her light eyes

and her gaze softened to warmth. Placing her arm about his waist, she gently helped him toward her cave. "Are all demons as gigantic as you?"

He snorted at her pertinent question. "Depends on the species. Some are small enough to fit in your palm." He sucked his breath in sharply as he stumbled on a hidden bramble, and pain hit him anew.

She didn't flinch as he put more weight on her than he'd meant to.

Amazed by her, he gentled his grip on her shoulder, not wanting to hurt her in any way. "Are all women as brave as you?"

Finally, a smile curved her lips, and it was as breath-taking a sight as he'd thought. "Depends on the species."

He'd arched a brow at her flippant, teasing tone. "Well, aren't you a cheeky one?"

"So says my father. It's ever a fault of mine that I don't know my place. But who better to know my place than I, says I? And who so better to determine it? For I will not be hemmed in by anyone else's expectations. This is my life, such as it is. And it will be lived under my rules and no one else's so long as I have it."

She led him into the dark cave where his sight quickly adjusted.

Even more surprised by her spirit that was unafraid of the dark he called home, he sat down on the floor while she went to a corner and uncovered a small tinder box. If he didn't know better, he'd think her part demon the way she moved about in the darkness as if she could see plainly.

But it was merely the fact that she was familiar with the place and knew where everything in it was put. She struck a flintstone and lit a small tallow candle to burn. Holding it aloft, she used it to light several more candles that were on the cave walls, then placed it in a small makeshift sconce she'd created.

Once she could see, she returned and knelt down by his side. When she reached for his stomach, he caught her soft hand with his claws. "What are you doing?"

She gave him a blank stare. "I was going to inspect your injury. Surely, you don't think I could do you harm?"

No, but trust didn't come easy for him. He'd never had anyone who hadn't sought in the past to give him all manner of pain.

That list included his own parents. So why should he give her any chance to do harm?

"I won't hurt you. I promise."

Those words amused him. It was like a gnat speaking to a lion. As if she could do anything...

So reluctantly, he loosened his grip and surrendered to her care. As promised, she didn't hurt him. Rather she carefully examined his wound then tore away a section of her underdress to bandage it.

That selfless act hit him twofold. One, that she destroyed her own dress for his care. And two, that her touch was feather-light and seared him to the core of his rotten soul.

When she was done, she sat back to smile down at him. "You lie still and rest. I shall get you something to eat and drink."

"Thank you."

"You're welcome..."

By the way she said that he knew she wanted something from him, but he had no idea what.

After a second, she laughed. "What's your name?"

"Malphas."

"Malphas?" she repeated in distaste. "That name doesn't suit you at all."

"How do you figure?"

"You're far too handsome to be a Malphas." She actually made a face as she said it.

Malphas gaped at her words. He was completely wearing his demon form in her presence. The one thing he'd learned early in his life was that humans hated whenever his kind wore their demon skins. Everything about his kind was repugnant to the human species.

Yet it didn't seem to faze her at all.

Not even the darkness of his blood or the length of his claws that had been designed to shred human flesh appeared to bother her. She acted as if he were as normal to her as daylight.

And it softened his hardened warrior's heart in a way nothing ever had before. "What name would you have for me, then, little one?"

She pursed her lips into an adorable frown as she considered it. Then, to his complete consternation, she reached up and gently brushed his orange hair back from his face so that she could cup his cheek and study his features. "Caleb."

It left him speechless that she'd instinctively picked a name so close to his summoning name that could enslave him to her... as if she could sense it somehow.

But more than that—

"Caleb?" He shuddered. "Why such an awful thing?"

She dropped her hand to the center of his chest. "Because I sense in you a true heart. A faithful heart. And by your wounds and scars, I can tell that you are fearless. So I shall call you Caleb, the faithful, fearless warrior who defends what he believes with everything he has. That is what I see when I look upon you. Not a demon. An ever courageous, noble warrior. One day, I suspect, you shall look into a mirror and see the same noble man I do."

And with that handful of words, she shattered the icy barrier that had caged his heart since the moment he'd been forsaken to this harsh bitter world without friend or family. "I can assure you that I will never look into a mirror and see a man there. At least not that I don't scream. Then kill it."

She laughed. "You know what I mean. Now let me see about collecting your sword before it's found, and they begin looking for you. Then I'll make sure you have supplies until you're well enough to rejoin your army."

His breath left him in a rush as he realized that he'd completely forgotten his weapon.

What the hell?

He'd never in his life set his sword aside. Never been disarmed by anyone.

Until now.

She had totally distracted him. He'd set it aside without a second a thought. What magick did this human wield so effortlessly that she could ensnare the most lethal demon commander in the entire Mavromino army?

For weeks now, he'd been pursued by their deadliest forces. Even wounded, he'd put down their best soldiers with minimal effort.

And she had done nothing more than smile and he'd laid aside his sword.

I'm an idiot.

Without another word, she headed for the entrance.

"Wait!"

A beautiful scowl drew her brows together. "Something wrong?"

"I don't know your name, girl."

An unbelievably beautiful smile melted away her frown. "Lilliana."

It was as remarkable as she was.

And with that, she vanished into the daylight.

Malphas lay there in complete shock. This had been the oddest day of his life.

He was trusting someone.

No, he was trusting a human.

Are you out of your mind?

Why would he have faith in her? Surely, she was going for the others to tell them where he was.

That made sense. She'd gone for his sword because it had been forged by the gods. Mortal weapons were worthless against him. To kill him, they needed *his* sword or magick.

You fool! She's probably leading them to you right now. With your sword in hand.

Get up!

Malphas had no doubt she was a spy. No human

could stand one such as he. It'd all been a lie. No one was that kind.

His head spinning, he forced himself to stand. The cave tilted.

He staggered toward the entrance.

There, he saw the strangest thing of all.

Lilliana was heading back toward him with his weapon in one hand, and a basket of food in the other.

Alone.

There was no one trailing behind her. No one following. He sensed nothing but her presence.

Could this be real? It seemed impossible and yet...

She was drawing nearer.

Not wanting her to know of his suspicions, he returned to where she'd left him, and sat back on the floor, ready to attack if need be.

Her face was flushed, and she was out of breath. "How do you carry this thing?"

"What?"

"Your sword. It weighs as much as a horse." Without a single reservation, she handed his sword hilt to him. "No wonder your muscles are so big. Should take a giant to wield it for battle."

He had no comment to that as he stared in awe of her innocence. She could have killed him. Or summoned others to do so.

Instead, she pulled out clothes, food and drink from her basket, then set about redressing his wound while he worked around her to dress himself.

Waiting until Caleb finished pulling his clothes on, Lilliana bit her lip as she saw the nasty, jagged wound that he didn't even seem to feel. She could only imagine how much it must burn. Yet he said nothing. Indeed, he acted as if he wasn't wounded at all.

Malphas. She knew that name. He was one of the generals who was against them.

No wonder he was feared. He was massively huge and terrifying to behold. Yet it wasn't that simple. There was a great beauty to his form. Granted, it was an unusual form. Still...

He was handsome in a peculiar way.

He's a demon!

Her father would beat her senseless if he ever learned she'd helped one of his kind. The village elder would kill her for daring to render aid.

So why are you risking your life for someone who spends his time killing humans?

She had no idea really, other than it was what she'd been taught. Help those in need. If someone was hungry, you should feed them. If they were wounded, you helped.

You know they never meant that for a demon.

True, but he didn't seem like a mindless raging animal. He was quite sentient.

Human-like.

She glanced at those eerie eyes that watched her so intently. "Does that hurt?"

"What?"

"Your eyes. They..."

"What?"

Lilliana wished she'd not said anything. But now that she had, she needed to finish it. "You seem to see more than I do."

He let out a bitter laugh. "Not true."

"How so?"

"I would have only seen an enemy and I would have killed it where it lay." He rubbed against the bandage she'd made. "I never would have rendered aid."

"Should I be afraid?"

The tenderness evaporated from his eyes. "Yes. You should. I'm a very dangerous thing."

"And I am not, Caleb. I'm trusting you to keep your word and not hurt me."

He curled his lip. "That name is atrocious."

"That name is quite beautiful, like you are. It's my favorite, in fact." Sitting back, she wrinkled her nose at him. "Do you have a favorite name?"

"Lilliana." It came out as a faint whisper that

shocked her and by the stunned expression on his face, she could tell he felt the same.

Clearing his throat, he sent his gaze toward his weapon. "May I ask another favor?"

"Of course."

"Could you hand my sword to me?"

That wasn't terrifying at all. Had she angered him so greatly? "May I ask why?"

"It needs to be cleaned."

"Oh." Lilliana hesitated as she finally realized how much blood coated it. "Was it a great battle?" Or had he slaughtered so many innocents? A tremor of fear and trepidation went through her. Had she assisted someone she shouldn't have?

He let out an elongated breath. "It was a tremendous battle."

"How did you survive it?"

Snorting, he gestured at his blood-soaked bandage. "I haven't yet."

She dragged the heavy sword to him. "I don't think your wounds are mortal."

A slight smile curved his lips. "It's not mortal wounds I fear, little mouse. It's immortal ones that will end me." He took the sword from her hand and used a portion of her bandage to clean the blade.

"Who were you fighting?"

"Not humans. Put your mind at ease. I normally pay no attention to your kind. I have better prey I prefer to slaughter ... those that can adequately fight back."

She wasn't sure if that comforted her or made it worse. "Are you saying you don't kill humans?"

He paused in the cleaning to pin her with an intense stare. "I kill anything that gets in my way. And definitely whatever attempts to kill me."

"Point taken, then. I shall stay out of your way."

Malphas lowered the sword. "I didn't mean that as a threat to you."

"It sounded like a threat."

"Then I'm sorry. I don't spend much time talking to others."

"Ah. I see."

He frowned at her. "What does that mean?"

"You're like my father. Too busy barking orders and opinions to be bothered with what others think ... or feel."

One corner of his mouth twitched as if he wanted to smile, but wouldn't allow himself to do so. "Do you fear anything?"

"You, my lord demon. You are terrifying."

"So you keep saying. Yet you don't act afraid."

"I beg to disagree."

He shook his head. "In my opinion, people in terror run away, screaming. They don't embrace their fear."

"I can't speak about how others behave. My father taught me that if you run, things will chase you. Therefore, you should stand strong and confront danger. Better to die trembling on your feet than screaming on your belly."

Malphas paused at the wisdom in those words. He'd never known a human like her. She might not be a warrior, but she held more courage than anyone he'd ever fought.

Indeed, it was easy to confront enemies when armed and trained. Another matter entirely to walk unarmed toward something you knew could gut you where you stood. She was truly fearless.

"Your father sounds interesting."

"He certainly thinks so." Eyes wide, she slapped her hand over her mouth as soon as she said that.

"Are you all right?"

"I didn't mean to say that. My father's a good man. Wise and kind. It was wrong of me to disparage him so."

Malphas laughed, amazed at the sound. Honestly, he couldn't remember the last time he'd done such. Too many years to even begin to count.

His laughter seemed to confuse her.

"Trust me, lady, that wasn't disparagement. Where I come from, we'd consider it a compliment."

"Then I'm sorry."

"For what?" he asked.

"It must be horrible to live in a place where insults are compliments."

Strange, he'd never thought about that before. It just was. He'd always accepted it as normal. "It's not horrible when you don't know better."

To his utter shock, she placed a gentle hand over his claw. "I wish, for your sake, that you'd known better." With a tender squeeze, she let go and stepped away from him.

Malphas wanted to be angry. Normally such a comment would have infuriated him to an impossible level. But he didn't want to induce terror in her, and that was the strangest part of all. He'd always reveled in his power to reduce those around him to tears or urination.

To watch them tremble in fear of his wrath.

There was no desire to do that to Lilliana. Instead, he wanted to hear her laughter. To see the light in her eyes glisten with mirth.

What is wrong with me?

Obviously, one too many hits to his head. He was battle-drunk. There was no other explanation.

Yeah, he'd accept that. It was a lot more palatable

than thinking she weakened him. Thinking there was something wrong with his black heart.

He watched as she headed for the entrance. "Are you leaving?"

Hesitating, she gathered her basket. "I must. If I'm gone too long, my father will come looking for me and since he knows I used to play here, he might inspect our cave. But I can return tomorrow with more food and medicine."

"That would be nice. Thank you." He said the words, but didn't mean them. Truth was, he didn't want her to leave.

Ever.

If his wing was working, he'd carry her off and dare her father to say a word.

But that would probably scare her and then she'd have no desire to be with him.

Or be kind.

If she were a demon, she'd kill him for even thinking such a thought. Involuntarily, he rubbed at the scar over his heart Lyseah had given him during one of their more amorous encounters. Pain and pleasure were synonymous to demons.

Does it have to be?

Malphas had never asked that question before. He'd taken pain as his birthright. Even though his father was a primal god, there had never been any sympathy for him. His mother had seen to that when she'd duped his father into impregnating her. It was a betrayal his primal god father had never forgiven and one he'd taken out on Malphas as if Malphas had a hand in his own conception.

Likewise, his demon mother had resented him for not causing an automatic bond between her and his father. Again, as if he were to blame for the fact that his father had no intention of being trapped by a demon out to use Jaden for all of his powers and influence.

That was the only thing Malphas didn't blame his father for. He more than understood his father's resistance to being controlled and used by those Jaden hated.

What he held against his father was Jaden's cold brutality where Malphas was concerned. Malphas hadn't asked to be conceived and he damn sure hadn't asked to be born. In truth, he'd have been better off had his father fried him the moment his mother had taken Malphas to him.

Instead, the entire world had spent the rest of his life making him pay for his parents' mistake.

Except for Lilliana. She knew nothing of his parentage. Nothing of his real tendencies.

To her, he was someone in need. A wounded beast to care for.

That still stunned him.

But like his father, he wasn't about to be used or tamed. Not by anyone.

He'd rest tonight. Tomorrow, he'd be gone before she returned. Back to his army.

Back to his war.

2

"Where are you going?"

Lilliana paused as she heard her father's strict demand that he framed as a question. Biting her lip, she quickly covered the items in her basket with a cloth and turned to face him. "I was going to gather herbs. Is there something you need?"

"You to stay home. They said in town that there was a demon spotted nearby. They're searching, but so far none have found him."

"When did they see it?"

"Yesterday."

She wrinkled her nose. "Then I'm sure the demon's long gone by now. Why would it stay?"

"You do have a point. They said it'd been wounded."

"Surely, it wouldn't stay here in such shape."

Her father scratched at his gray beard. "Perhaps not."

"Then there's nothing to fear. I shall return soon."

He growled at her. "One day I fear I shall come to regret indulging you so."

"You said that yesterday and the day before."

"Impudent child! Go. Gather your herbs, but if you're not back within an hour, I'll fetch you back myself."

She gave him a sarcastic salute. "Aye, sir. I'll return forthwith."

Adjusting the basket on her arm, she quickly swept out of their cottage before he realized what she carried wasn't empty. Yet she kept looking over her shoulder in fear of being followed or spotted.

If they were still looking for her demon, they could easily stumble on her cave. That wouldn't bode well for any of them. While she wanted to believe Caleb wouldn't harm them, she wasn't a fool. The last thing she wanted was to see the blood of someone she knew smeared on his sword.

So, she made her way carefully to where she'd left him.

As she entered the cave, she looked around. For

some reason, Caleb hadn't started a fire. Maybe he didn't know how?

Maybe he didn't need one.

"Caleb?"

No one answered. Worried, she moved forward until her eyes adjusted.

Then, she saw him on the ground with his wings spread out.

Terrified and breathless, she rushed to his side. He was burning with a fever.

"Caleb?" she asked again.

Again, he didn't answer.

Lilliana blamed herself for leaving him. But he'd seemed so incredibly strong. Invincible even.

What did one do for a demon with a fever? She had no idea. Maybe they were the same as a human?

It was the only place she knew to start. Scrambling for her basket, she pulled her supplies free and quickly used the cold water to try and draw out the fever.

Thankfully, she had stopped along her way to pick some herbs... just in case her father checked.

Garlic. Sage... rosemary. They might help. Mixing them together, she made a fast poultice for his festering wound. Her stomach tightened as she saw how much worse it was today. The ragged edges were awful, letting her know that whoever had delivered the wound had intended to kill him.

Stupid thought really. Of course, they'd meant to kill him. It'd been a battle. The very thought saddened her. She didn't like war, and this battle between gods, demons and men had been going on for far too long. Longer than she'd been alive.

Why wouldn't they find peace? Her father called her foolish for such thoughts. Maybe she was. Because really, the world was a large place. Surely, there was room for everyone?

It just didn't make sense to her.

Carefully, she redressed his wound.

Hissing, he swatted at her as if she were an annoying fly.

"Shh, Caleb. It's only me." Her hand brushed against the taut skin of his abdomen.

He came awake with a curse. For a second, his eyes and body appeared human, then they returned to their eerie demon-snake eyes and flaming red skin. "Lilliana?"

"Aye."

Scowling, he rubbed at his forehead. "What happened?"

"You've a fever. I think you might have passed out." She reached for her basket and took the bread, meat and cheese from it. "I brought you something to eat and drink."

Malphas wanted to curse her for that kindness, but honestly, he was grateful. It'd been a long time since he'd been wounded this severely. A long time since he'd passed out.

Had she not hidden him...

He would most likely have been found. If not by the humans, then by those who wanted him dead.

This frail, tiny human had saved his life... he couldn't believe it.

You need to leave.

He couldn't. Not when her light eyes glistened in the dim light and looked at him as if he were...

Human.

Really, it should offend him with every ounce of his being. And maybe it would have had he not been running a heavy fever. As it was...

He wanted to feel her hands on his skin again. *Yeah, I am burning a fever.* He had to be out of his mind to want something like that. What he needed was to get back to his life. Back to the dimly lit realm he called home and fight in the war he dominated.

It was all he knew. What he understood.

"You should drink some water."

He paused at her gentle voice. "What?"

"Water will help with your fever." She handed him a small skin.

"Thank you."

She smiled sweetly. "I should also let you know that my father said there are men searching for you."

That caught his attention. "Are they?"

"Aye. But I didn't see them on my way here. I think they're looking elsewhere, but I wanted you to be careful."

Malphas felt his injured wing twitch. He couldn't fly home with that wing— at least not in this body. Using his powers, he changed into a raven.

Lilliana gasped.

Ignoring her, he tried to stretch his wounded wing. It was as useless in this form as when he'd been a demon.

Damn. Frustrated and angry, he returned back into his preferred form. He couldn't even teleport.

"How do you do that?"

He blinked at her awed question. "Do what?"

"Change from one body to another?"

Malphas shrugged. "How do you not?"

"It's not natural for us. I'd love to have that ability."

He glanced down at the claws on his hands. "It's not so impressive." Then he met her wide-eyed gaze and confessed a truth he'd never told anyone else. "Neither one is my real form."

Her eyes widened. "What?"

He ran his tongue along his fangs. Over the centuries, he'd grown so used to them that he forgot at times this wasn't the body he'd been born into. The real form he'd default to if he hadn't made staying a demon his priority.

It'd taken him years to master remaining in his Daeve body, especially while he was sleeping.

Now, it was second nature.

But if he were to die, he'd revert to the form he'd held at birth. It was an image that he never showed to anyone.

He *hated* it.

So why was he changing into it now?

"Caleb!" Lilliana breathed as she watched his skin fade from blood red to a beautiful tawny color. His yellow eyes turned dark brown and his hair became as black as night. Never had she seen a more handsome man.

To her utter shock, he passed a sheepish smile to her. "This is what I really look like."

Breathless, she reached out slowly to touch his whiskered cheek. "Why would you hide such beauty?"

"I look like my father, and I hate him with every begrudging breath I draw in."

"You shouldn't let him steal any part of you. If you

hate him so, then waste no time worrying about him, his ideas, or his looks. Otherwise, he owns that part of you for free. Don't let him have it."

"Huh..." Malphas had never thought of it that way. Especially given that he'd always hated and resented his father. He didn't think of it as being possessive, it just was.

But Lilliana was right. It did allow his father to dominate an area of his life and dictate his behavior.

Screw Jaden.

With a smile, Lilliana leaned forward. "I would never hide such beauty. You're amazing."

"Amazing enough for a kiss?" He'd meant it as a flippant taunt.

She didn't take it that way. Wrinkling her nose, she leaned forward and innocently placed her lips against his.

Malphas smiled at what had to be the most chaste kiss he'd ever known. She tasted of warmth and sweetness. Of everything he'd been denied in his life.

Of everything he'd ever wanted. He deepened the kiss, amazed even more that it didn't scare her. Amazed that she welcomed his touch.

How?

He was evil incarnate. Held no regard for anyone or

anything. He'd picked his teeth with the bones of humans twice her size.

You hate them.

But there was no hate inside him for this woman. Tiny as she was, she crippled him.

You need to push her away.

How could he? He was desperate to feel her beside him. And then the most shocking thing of all happened.

His side healed. Gasping, he felt his wings burst out of his back. Like his side, his injured wing was back to normal. No pain. Not even a ruffled feather.

No... it wasn't possible. Granted he normally healed much faster than humans, but this...

How? It didn't make any sense whatsoever. He didn't have the powers to heal. Malphas was a creature of utter destruction.

Chaos.

Your father can heal.

True. As a god of light, Jaden held the powers of creation and healing. Malphas had thought that was beyond him.

Until now.

"What have you done to me?"

She blinked innocently. "I don't understand?"

He pulled the bandage away to show her that not even a scar remained. "I'm healed."

With an adorable gape, she gently fingered his abdomen. "It's a miracle."

It was something he didn't understand. "Have you any powers?"

She was aghast at his question. "No. Why?"

Not wanting to let her know how much control she had over him, he cleared his throat. "The humans who were after me... they had a sorcerer in their midst."

"Orus."

"You know him?"

"Only by reputation. He's a fierce warrior. Feared by everyone."

Malphas bit back a snort. "I only wondered if you had such powers, too."

"My only power is irritating my father." Suddenly, she was nervous. "And speaking of, I'd best head home before he starts searching for me."

Something inside him screamed out a denial at the thought of her leaving. Especially when she spoke her next sentence. "I guess you'll be leaving now, huh?"

Made sense. He had no reason to stay. But there was a foreign ache inside him he didn't understand. The thought of leaving actually caused him pain.

And by the sadness in her eyes, he wondered if she felt it, too.

"I'm sure you'll be glad to see me gone."

Lilliana shook her head as her eyes became glassy. "I think I'll miss you, Caleb. I wish you could stay."

Those words should anger him. Make him curse her. Instead, he brushed the pale hair back from her cheek. "What if I could?"

Her eyes widened, then her entire face lit up. "Really? Could you?"

You're a fool. Don't even think it!

Malphas had always hated that inner voice that constantly nagged and berated him.

This time, it was right. He shouldn't have any of the thoughts that were in his head. He had an army to command. A war to fight.

And a beautiful woman in front of him who caused the strangest feelings inside him.

There will always be a battle and war.

True. It was the nature of the gods to fight. Man even more so. Demons lived for conflict. Nature of the beasts.

But how often would he have a gentle woman staring up at him like this?

Screw it. If he had to die, he'd rather it be with Lilliana than fighting for a cause he didn't believe in or care about. Rising to his feet, he dressed himself like the humans who'd been chasing after him, then held his hand out for her. "Can I walk you home?"

Taking his hand, she allowed him to pull her to her

feet. "Of course, you can, kind sir." Her gaze went to his sword. "But that might beg more questions than either of us can answer."

Malphas used his telekinesis to pick up and strap it to this back.

"Where did it go?"

Malphas grinned. "It's still here. Hidden in plain sight."

Lilliana just stared at him.

"What?" he asked, curious about the expression on her face.

"You... I just can't get over how incredible you look in your real body. I mean, you were handsome as a demon, but like this... it's unbelievable."

Maybe, but what he considered unbelievable was being here with her.

I'm an absolute idiot.

And like a dutiful puppy, he followed her home to find the father she was so afraid of. Old and gray, he had a pair of piercing blue eyes. While that might scare a human, Malphas wanted to laugh. The man had no idea who he was addressing.

More to the point, what he was addressing.

Her father raked a less than becoming sneer over Malphas, even though Malphas was a full head and shoulders taller than he was. "Where'd you pick up a stray, Lilli?"

"I was peeing on a tree when she passed by me."

Her father arched a brow. "Beg pardon?"

Lilliana shook her head. "Caleb's teasing you, Papa. He tends to do that around strangers."

"Well, he's not welcome here. Go sniff around someone else's daughter."

Lilliana let out a tired breath. "You said you needed help with the barn. Can he not work for food and shelter?"

The old man looked as if he were having bowel problems. Finally, he scratched at his beard. "You know how to build anything?"

Not really. He was better at setting fire to buildings. "I can manage."

"Then you can sleep in the barn. That'll motivate you to fix the roof as quickly as possible." He turned to look at his daughter. "And you'll find your chores keep you in the cottage while he's here."

A beautiful blush darkened her cheeks. "Yes, Papa."

Clearing his throat, her father led her to their cottage and then showed Malphas to the barn. "You can make a bed on the straw."

"Thank you, sir."

As Malphas stepped away, her father stopped him. "Look, I'm no fool. Me daughter's not the most beautiful of girls, but she's innocent and I won't have the likes of you trifling with her. You understand me?"

Those words awoke the demon inside him. It took everything he had not to cut the man down where he stood. The only thing that stayed his sword arm was the knowledge that Lilliana loved her father and would be heartbroken if Malphas killed the old geezer.

"You, sir, do your daughter a grave injustice. She is the most beautiful woman I've ever beheld. I would do nothing to harm her or her reputation. Have no fear there." Malphas took a step forward. "But know this, I won't have you ever disparage her, either. As you said, she's innocent and holds the kindest heart I've ever known."

Her father stood bravely, but Malphas could smell the fear he was trying desperately to hide. "Where are you from?"

"Azmodea."

"Never heard of it."

"It's in the south." The far south as it was a hell realm where no sun was allowed to shine. Sadly, it was where his mother had dumped him once she realized his father would have nothing to do with a half-demon son.

"What brings you here?"

"Happenstance. I was passing through until I met Lilliana."

Her father's nostrils flared. "Then perhaps you should keep passing through."

"Papa!" Lilliana's panicked scream made Malphas's heart race.

He ran past her father to see what was wrong.

She was in the yard, surrounded by a group of men. Malphas slowed as he saw the sorcerer among them. Tall and slender, he was hard to miss.

So was the way they were shouting at her.

"What did you see, girl?"

"Where is it?"

"What were you doing?"

"Are you possessed?"

"Did you speak to the demon?"

They spoke over each other so fast that it was hard to discern their individual questions. Lilliana had her hands over her ears as she tried to shrink away from them.

But they wouldn't let her. With every backward step she made, they took two toward her.

"Papa!" The panic and fear in her voice caused his powers to surge.

How dare they scare her so. His heart racing, Malphas advanced on them. "Leave her alone!"

The men turned to fight, until they realized how tall he was. How much more muscled. There was no mistaking the fear and reservation in their eyes as they stepped back to clear a path between Malphas and Lilliana. He didn't pause until he stood with his back to her so that he could shield her from the eight men.

He could feel her relief. Especially when she placed a trembling hand on his back. "Thank you," she whispered.

Malphas didn't respond. Instead, he glared at the group. "What do you want?"

Orus, the sorcerer, stepped forward. "Information."

"About?"

An old man to Orus's right scratched at his chin. "We saw her footsteps. She's been going to a cave not far from where a demon was sighted. We want to know why she was there and if she saw the demon we're after."

Malphas saw the terror on her father's face. Luckily, he stood behind the others so that they couldn't see his expression. The demonic part of him wanted to set fire to them all. He didn't owe them any kind of explanation and neither did she.

Sadly, he was acutely aware of her hand at his hip. The fear she had as she held on to his cloak.

Forcing the demon inside him down, he faced them with a sneer. "I was in the cave."

"Why?"

"Had a run-in with a demon." It wasn't really a lie. The Sephirii were demons to his kind. And they could be just as harmful to humans.

More so, actually.

The men were now in awe. "Are you a warrior?"

"How are you alive?"

"What happened?"

"Where's the demon?"

Again, their voices blurred together. And Malphas didn't miss the suspicious light in Orus's eyes. Yet beneath that was another glimmer. One that made the hair on the back of his neck stand up.

"I'm a demigod, and I dispatched your demon. For a price." Again, it was all true. So long as he was in this form, his demonic half was quelled.

The price just happened to be...

Honestly, he wasn't sure. But there was always a price to everything. Good. Bad. Indifferent. Happiness and sorrow. It all took a toll.

Orus eyed him with his own sneer. "If you're a demigod, who's your father?"

"Verlyn." It was the name humans used for his father, Jaden.

That caused the ones closest to him to gasp.

"Truly?" the old man asked.

"Aye, and I wouldn't claim it if it wasn't true. We're not exactly friendly with each other. And he's not merciful to anyone who lies about having a connection to him." Jaden had been known to set imposters on fire. Pull out eyes. Testicles.

On his good days.

In a bad mood...

Well, no one wanted to be around his father in a bad mood. Not even his father. And Malphas never wanted to be around his father in any given situation.

"If you're a demigod, prove it."

Malphas stared at Orus as if the sorcerer was the biggest idiot ever born. Which he'd have to be to pose such a question. None of Malphas's ilk like to be challenged, especially not by petty humans.

"And how would you like me to prove it? Rain? Fire? Or..." He pulled his sword from his back and lifted the invisibility cloak.

All of the group stepped back in awe. Orus moved forward to inspect it.

Until Malphas ran fire along the blade. That caused the sorcerer to step back in fear.

"Why are you here?" Orus glanced to Lilliana.

"One good favor deserves another." He glanced over his shoulder to give her a smile.

"And where's the demon's body?"

Malphas arched a brow. Manifesting a ball of fire, he sent it flying into the nearby woods. "I destroyed it." Again, it was mostly true. So long as he remained in this form, his demon body was gone. Ergo, destroyed.

He smirked at the group. "Any more stupid questions?"

Shaking their heads, they began dispersing.

All except Orus. "Thank you for assisting us." Then, he turned away to follow after the others.

Lilliana's father came forward slowly. His gaze went to his daughter, then to Malphas. "Demigod?"

"Not exactly something I disclose when I first meet someone."

Still, he looked a little pale. "Why are you here?"

"I don't know," Malphas answered honestly. "I should go home to my realm, but I rather like it here. I've never spent much time in the human realm."

Her father snorted. "Not much to recommend it."

Malphas glanced at Lilliana as she stepped to his side. "I disagree."

"And they'll be none of that! I know all about you gods coming down here to impregnate our daughters."

She blushed at her father's command.

Malphas took her hand into his. "As I already told you, old man, I would *never* harm your daughter or her reputation."

Not like I could stop you anyway.

Malphas arched his brow as he heard her father's thoughts. At least the mortal was wise enough to know the truth.

"What exactly are your intentions for my daughter?"

Malphas turned to face her. "That is entirely up to her."

3

Lilliana paused as she watched Caleb come down from the roof. She still couldn't believe that he was here. For over two months, he'd helped her and her father with chores, and had slept happily in the barn.

'Course, the barn had never looked better. While her father had intended to make Caleb's stay there motivation to fix the roof, Caleb had gone far beyond those expectations. The barn had never looked better. There was even an addition that served as Caleb's bedroom. It was quite impressive.

And he'd done it all by the sweat of his own brow. Not once had Caleb resorted to his powers. He'd learned that he actually liked working with his hands.

Creating rather than destroying.

"Any idiot or monster can tear something down. It takes vision, intelligence, and talent to create out of thin air." She could still see the satisfaction on his face when he'd said those words to her.

He smiled as she joined him by his side. "I brought you some water." She held the cup in her hand out toward him.

"Thank you."

She took his hand into hers. "You've scraped your knuckles."

"A little bit."

Little bit, nothing. That had to hurt.

She shook her head, amazed by him. "I can't believe you actually do this by hand." His powers were such that he could blink and do it.

"Doesn't make sense to me, either. But I rather like working. It's good to create and I've never made anything before." He gave her a strange look. "Other than corpses."

"Caleb!" She both loved and hated whenever he teased her so. Loved the fact that he felt comfortable enough to be honest, but hated some of the facts of his past that he relayed. That being said, he'd come a long way.

And she deeply loved him for that. Killing was no longer his automatic response for all grievances.

But as much as she loved him, she knew that sooner or later he'd head home.

What was she going to do then? She couldn't imagine a day without his sarcasm and humor. As irritated as it could make her, she actually looked forward to it.

And he was a good listener. He never judged her or made her feel bad about anything. No matter how unorthodox her thoughts.

With an adorable smile, he handed her the cup she'd brought. "I better get back to work before your dad accuses me of making eyes at you again."

Laughing, she headed back toward their cottage.

Malphas watched as Lilliana headed inside. In truth, he wanted to follow after her and make sure to lock her father out.

That would only get them both in trouble.

Something he felt as soon as he returned to the roof where her father was waiting with more straw. "Didn't think to bring me any water, did you?"

"Uh..."

Ophelos laughed. "Think nothing of it. I'm just messing with you." He clapped Malphas on the back. "I'm more perturbed me daughter forgot she has a father up here sweating."

When had they become so comfortable that the old

man would touch him in such a friendly manner? It should scare him.

But strangely, he liked it.

Malphas returned to his work. After several minutes, he paused as he realized Ophelos was staring at him. "There a problem?"

"When are you going to ask me for me daughter's hand?"

Malphas blinked. Then blinked again. Had the old man actually said what he heard? "Pardon?"

"I'm not stupid, boy. Why else would one of your ilk still be here after all these months? I know what you can do. And I can only imagine the palace you probably call home. Why would you give that up to stay in me barn?"

That was a complicated answer. "I don't live in a palace." Honestly, his accommodations were only slightly better than the barn.

"You're a demigod."

"Whose father hates him."

"What of your mother?"

"Don't know. Could be dead. Rather hope she is." Malphas had no idea why he was confiding in the old man. It wasn't really like him to share such things. But then he'd grown used to saying such things to Lil. Maybe his new lippy openness was an extension of being around her. Made as much sense as any other explanation.

"You hate your mother?"

"No. That's too strong an emotion for someone you've never really known. I feel nothing toward her. She dumped me off on my father, then went on with her life as if I didn't exist."

"That must have been hard on your father."

"Not really. He dumped me off on one of his priestesses to raise. But at least he'd come around from time to time." Mostly to make sure Malphas wasn't giving in to his demonic urges.

Or to punish him for giving in to his demonic urges.

He definitely hated his father. That, he could never deny.

"So you've never had a family." It was a statement and not a question.

"I have one now." That fell out of his mouth before he could recall it.

He expected Ophelos to be angry at him for saying such a thing. But instead, he gave him a kindly smile. "Is that why you're staying on here?"

"I like being a part of something." Other than war and an army where he stood apart from his soldiers. They begrudged him his rank and resented the fact that his father was a god. He'd always felt as if he walked around them with a target on his back.

Here, he didn't have to guard himself at all times. Neither Lil nor Ophelos made comments that were meant to let blood or compliments that were actually veiled insults.

"So again, I ask you... what are your intentions with me daughter?"

"I would love to marry her. Nothing would give me greater pleasure."

Ophelos smiled. "Then you should ask her. Sooner rather than later."

That was easier said than done. Malphas lived in fear that Itzal or one of the others would come seeking him. There was no telling what they would do if they found him here.

With her.

It'd be a disaster for the humans. Especially if his demon brethren realized the reason for his absence.

Lilliana.

They'd kill her instantly. If for no other reason than to force him home.

Lyseah would kill her out of sheer jealousy. Even though there were no real feelings between him and Lyseah. Her spite and treachery would demand Lil's head. And he'd be forced to kill Lyseah. Hopefully before she killed the woman he loved.

Don't even think about it.

His kind were cursed by the gods. They weren't supposed to fall in love and...

Repair roofs.

He was a warrior, not a farmer. Yet this little farm brought him more happiness than he'd ever known existed. How could he walk away from that?

From her?

A motion below caught his eye. Lil was walking to the well to draw more water. The sight of her in that pale green gown made his heart quicken. She was the most beautiful creature in all existence.

Marry her.

Ophelos cleared his throat. "You know Pholos?"

"The shriveling pathetic wastrel from the village? I've seen him from time to time."

"He's asked me for Lilli's hand."

Malphas froze as that familiar rage took root in his soul. He could feel the heat of it invading his eyes.

Ophelos scrambled back. "I didn't tell him he could."

"Good." Malphas heard the deepening of his voice that never boded well for others.

"I didn't want to upset you, Caleb. I only wanted to

let you know that because you have taken a notice of her, others have, too."

And they could kiss his—

"Caleb?" Lilliana's voice cut through his thoughts as if she knew what he was thinking.

"Aye, love?" he called down to her.

She blew him a kiss. "Wanted you to know that I'm missing you."

That gesture...

There were no words for what it did to him. What it made him feel. But then that was the true beauty of her. She could leave him weak with nothing more than a glance. Good thing no one else could render him so helpless so effortlessly.

Ophelos nudged his arm. "You have the same look on your face that I wore every time I saw her mother. As much as it grieves me to think of me daughter with a man, I'd rather she be with one who'll treasure her than one who seeks only to have a servant to keep his house and bear his children. She deserves someone who knows how special she is."

And that she was. Malphas couldn't deny it.

Without saying a word, he left the roof to go after her.

She was in the cottage, pouring water into the

cistern. He swept up behind her so that he could pull her against his chest.

"That better be Caleb behind me."

He smiled at her indignant tone. "Aye. Anyone else would be gutted on the floor."

Laughing, she reached up to cup his face while he nuzzled against her neck. "You best be careful. My father is surely not far behind you."

"No doubt, but I think he'll give us a few more moments."

"What makes you think that?"

Malphas moved around so that he could stand in front of her. "Because I'm here to ask you to marry me."

Lilliana stared at him, unsure if she'd heard those words correctly. "Pardon?"

He cupped her hand in his and placed a tender kiss on her palm. "Marry me, Lil. Make me the happiest demon who's ever been born."

Happiness overwhelmed her to the point that all she could do was laugh and nod. Then she threw herself against him and held him tight.

Laughing, Caleb lifted her up off her feet and swung her about.

The door opened.

Still in Caleb's arms, she saw her father shaking his head. "I take it that you asked her."

Caleb slid her down the front of him until her feet were returned to the floor. Even so, he kept her cradled in his arms. "Indeed, I did."

"By the looks of her, I assume she said yes."

Lilliana wiped at the tears in her eyes. "Of course, I did."

"Good. Now I don't have to watch you mope about whenever Caleb's in the barn. So, when are you two planning this ceremony?"

Smiling, she reached up to smooth down a curl on Caleb's forehead. "Solstice."

Caleb frowned at her decree, as if a bad feeling went through him. "Why then?"

"It's the mark of a new year. New beginnings. Rebirth. All the wonderful celebrations. What better time to marry and start our life together?"

He visibly cringed. "It's the longest night of the year. Portals open. Bad things can walk in this world. Seems like we're tempting fate."

She tsked at him. "Ever the optimist, eh?"

Malphas wanted to argue, but he knew how much she wanted this date. How could he deny her anything, especially something so simple?

Still, he hated solstice. Too many of the demons he knew used it to their best advantage so that they could prey on humans.

But if it would make her happy...

"What can I say, Lil? There's only so much changing I'm capable of. I have to keep something of my old ways. Otherwise, you might not recognize me and go off with someone else thinking he's me."

With an impish smile, she kissed the tip of his nose. "I will always know my best friend. You can't hide from me."

But over the next six weeks as they headed into the solstice, Malphas was tempted to not only hide from her, but to run back to his hell realm to escape all the preparations she was making. It was ridiculous.

There were so many details. He'd never dreamed humans would torture themselves like this.

Who needed demons to terrorize their lives?

But he didn't want to live that way anymore. He much preferred their innocent, simple life than all the glory he'd received battling against humanity.

Humans weren't the despicable animals he'd once thought they were. They actually had a lot in common with his brethren. True, some were weasels. Yet compared to demons and their powers, the human weasels were tolerable.

All in all, he'd much rather live among them than either the gods or demons who'd birthed him.

"Wishing yourself back home?"

Caleb snorted at Ophelos's question. "Aye. I much prefer our cottage to this crowd."

Ophelos laughed. "I meant your former home, not our little place."

"I'll never wish myself back there."

That was what he said. However, the thronging mass of humans around him was very similar to the court at Azmodea. They were laughing, dancing and drinking as if this was their last night on earth. Or in the case of Azmodea, as if they were planning on a slaughter come dawn.

Those jubilant behaviors made him very apprehensive. Without thinking, he reached for Lilliana to keep her close and make sure she was safe.

"Isn't it amazing?"

Caleb wouldn't call it that. "Sure. Drunken vomit always excites me." He pulled her to the left, away from just such a nasty splash.

"Well, okay, that's not the great part. And thank you for saving my shoes and dress."

"Ever my pleasure to save you." Especially given how beautiful she was in them. The light yellow made her blue eyes glow with warmth. She looked like a perfect confection that made his mouth water.

For that alone, he was willing to suffer through the vendors, acrobats and drunken revelers that surrounded them. And dodging the hands of strange women they passed who kept wanting to dance with him.

She scowled at one and set the woman back on her heels with an actual hiss. "Maybe this wasn't such a good idea."

Arching his brow, he turned toward Lil. "Pardon?"

"I don't like the way women are looking at you."

"Makes two of us." He gently grabbed her waist and held her right in front of him. "Save me, love. I need you to keep them away."

"Oh trust me. If any one of them comes near you, she'll walk away bald."

Wrapping his arms around her, he pulled her to a stop so that he could lay his cheek against the top of her head. "That's my fierce little mouse."

He gave her a light squeeze before he let go and she danced off toward the temple where the priest would be waiting for them. Caleb actually had to quicken his steps to catch up to her.

When they entered the temple, they were laughing and stumbling.

Until the priest gave them a stern glower. "Do you know where you are?"

Caleb snorted. "My father's temple," he whispered in her ear.

Lil laughed, then forced herself to stop. "Aye, Lord Priest. Please forgive us. We meant no disrespect."

"Not true," he whispered in her ear.

She elbowed him in the stomach. "Caleb!"

"Is there no other temple in this village? Must we really marry here?"

The priest stiffened visibly. "Have you a problem with Lord Verlyn?"

He had so, so many. Honestly, he didn't even know where to begin to describe all the problems he had with his father. That could take decades, maybe even centuries to recount.

But that thought vanished as he caught sight of someone in the shadows of his father's hideous statue.

Myone.

Stunned, he stepped back from Lil. A part of him wanted to run. No, it needed to run. *Why did I agree to this?*

To make Lil happy. She'd wanted it to be in his father's temple, hoping to placate his father and reunite them.

Caleb had agreed only because he knew his father would never bother coming to such a place. Jaden honestly didn't care.

But he had forgotten that his father had a penchant for sending acolytes out to gather his tributes and bring them home. After all, his ego was even larger than that statue towering over them, and his father wanted to see the offerings of those who worshipped him because they had no idea what an asshole Jaden actually was.

Of all the sycophants who'd latched on to his sperm donor, Myone was the last one he'd have expected to run into for such a petty mission. As the leader of the Sephirii army, she should have much more important things to attend.

And given the size of her belly, she should be in labor any moment now. How many months were they pregnant? Nineteen-hundred?

Then again, she hadn't been showing last time.

Maybe that was why she was here. She was way too pregnant for battle.

"I'll be right back," he whispered to Lil before he started toward his enemy.

Myone eyed him cautiously.

He expected her to flee at his approach.

Instead, she stood her ground and eyed him warily. "What are you doing here, Malphas?"

"Paying respects. You?"

"I think you know." She started around him, but he stopped her.

Malphas gasped as he touched her and saw a future image of what her son would look like.

What he'd do.

In the future, he was fighting under Jaden's banner. Given how much his brother hated their father, he found it impossible that Xev's son would fight for the grandfather who'd done so much harm to them.

"Does Xevikan know about the baby?"

"Shh!" she snapped before looking about as if terrified someone would overhear them. "You know nothing. I carry your brother. Not your brother's son."

"What game are you playing?"

"I'm not a demon. I don't play games with people."

She might be saying that, but he knew better. Had his father impregnated her, the baby wouldn't have the stench of the Mavromino on it. It was unmistakable. Xevikan's mother was the Queen of All Darkness. Azura. He'd served his aunt long enough to know her unique brand of evil, and Myone's child reeked of it.

"Does Xev know?" he asked again.

The sadness in her eyes actually wrung pain from his heart. She didn't respond with words. Just a subtle nod.

Caleb winced. "Let me guess. Marrying you off to our father was his idea to protect the baby."

"To protect me."

Caleb ground his teeth. Of course. His brother was an even bigger idiot than he'd assumed. "You two are playing with fire." If they thought for one moment they could fool his father, they were stupid beyond belief.

"You know Jaden is smarter than this."

"I know. He's never touched me, and my lord has no intention of touching me. He's said as much."

"Does Braith know?"

She frowned at him. "I don't know. Why would you ask that?"

Talk about playing with fire...

"When she had an affair with her Sephiroth, they demanded Kissare's life as punishment. If Jaden doesn't take your life in the same manner, Braith will be even more hate-filled than she already is."

The war they were fighting would worsen and become bloodier than anyone could imagine.

"I didn't know about that."

But his father did. How could anyone forget Braith's wrath? It was a large part of what had led to this war. She wanted the lives of everyone who'd forced the death of her love.

Mostly, that short list was his father, Cam and Rezar. And his aunt, Lilith, just because.

So long as they breathed, Braith intended to back Azura and Noir in their fight. To watch the world burn. And Caleb should know. Braith was his primary commander.

Her and her son, Monakribos Malachai. The head demon boss. Everything went from Braith to her son to Caleb.

No wonder he was so much happier with the humans than with his evil overlords.

Myone looked past his shoulder to where Lilliana waited for him. "There's something different about you, Malphas." She swept her gaze over his humble human clothes. "And I don't just mean the downgrade on your wardrobe. You seem almost... nice."

He hated that it showed, and he wanted to lie to her. But he couldn't. "Can I ask a favor?"

She arched a brow. "Last time we were together, you tried to kill me."

"And you almost succeeded in killing me." One corner of his mouth lifted in an amused grin. "Thank you for that."

"Sarcasm?"

"Truth. I owe you, Myone. Anything you ever need."

Her frown turned to confusion. "Then why are you asking me for a favor?"

"Because I don't want anyone to know where I am. You keep my secret and I'll keep yours."

"I don't understand."

"Caleb?"

He winced as Lilliana finally approached them.

Suspicion clouded her pale eyes and he hated that he'd put it there. He'd never hurt her. Not intentionally.

"Is something wrong?"

He tried to think of something to say. Something to keep her from learning about Myone. But he didn't want to lie to her. "I was talking to my sister. Myone meet Lilliana."

Myone gasped. "I was right. There is something different about you, Malphas."

"Caleb," he corrected before her father or the priest overheard them.

"Are you here for our wedding?" Lil asked.

"Wedding?" Myone's gaze went from Caleb to Lilliana and back again. "So you do have a heart."

"Myone... please."

"Have no fear, Malphas. I'd never harm an innocent. I'm not the demon here."

Her barb irritated him, but he wasn't about to break their truce. "Yet you wouldn't hesitate to harm me. I still have the scar in my side to prove it."

Lil sucked her breath in sharply. "She's the one who wounded you?"

"She is. But I forgive her. It was the kindest thing anyone ever did for me before I met you."

Lilliana was aghast at his nonchalance. "Your sister tried to kill you?" Furious at the very thought, she turned on the tall, graceful woman. "Why would you do such a thing? How could you?"

"He's a..." Myone stopped as if she thought better of what she was about to say. Then, she passed a scowl toward Caleb. "You do know the difference between you and your brother?"

"My demon blood." It was all any of their kind ever saw when they looked at him. "But I'll take demonic blood over Azura's any day. And need I remind you that Xev isn't a demigod. He's a full god of chaos, plagues, violent death... should I continue?"

Myone held her hand up. "I'm well aware of his flaws."

"Yet you love him anyway."

Shaking her head, she turned back to Lilliana. "There's something profoundly wrong with us that we allowed such reprobates into our hearts." With a kind smile, she placed a kiss on Lilliana's brow. "I'm glad to have you as my sister." Then, she faced Caleb. "Don't make me regret my silence."

He took Lilliana's hand and made her blush as he placed a tender kiss on her palm. "I'm not the demon you fought. I'll never be him again."

"Good. Now, I need to give you a gift."

"Your silence is all I ask."

Myone smiled at Caleb. With a wave of her hand,

she changed his clothes into the elegant robes of a noble lord. Then, she snapped her fingers and Lilliana found herself in a light blue dress made of the finest, softest material she'd ever touched.

Running her hand over it, she couldn't believe the way it felt on her skin. "What is this?"

"Silk."

The priest neared them. "What's going on?"

Myone turned to face the old man. "This young couple has the blessings and benediction of our Lord Verlyn. They are very special to him. He will smile kindly upon your ceremony. Please take care of them."

The priest's face lit up. "Really?"

Myone nodded. "Absolutely."

"Laying it on a bit thick, sister?"

She clapped Caleb on the arm. "At least I'm not stabbing you this time. Take it as a win."

"Any day I'm not bleeding, inside or out, I take as a win." And with that, he pulled Lilliana gently toward the altar.

Caleb scowled up at the statue. "He looks nothing like that."

Lilliana bit her lip. "How so?"

"For one thing, it's not sneering at me. Another, he has long hair and sharp features." He lifted himself up on his toes and curled his lip. "This is what he normally looks like."

She laughed at the exaggerated face he made. "Be nice, my love. He might be watching."

"Doubtful. I'm his least favorite child."

The priest joined them and placed two wreaths on their heads. Festival wreaths made of dried greenery someone had interwoven with holly berries. Not the most comfortable headdress, but Caleb didn't mind. Especially given how lovely Lilliana looked in hers.

Lighting candles, the priest motioned for Myone and Ophelos to move closer. "Let our witnesses step forward to behold a sacred union."

Caleb saw the two of them and then he caught movement from the corner of his eye. Turning his head, he felt his jaw go slack at the presence of his brother, Xev.

He met Myone's gaze. Smiling bashfully, she moved to stand with him.

Caleb didn't know what to think. But a wave of guilt went through him. He hadn't been there for them, and he didn't understand their kindness toward him now. Until Lilliana, kindness of any kind had been unknown. He'd never understood it or felt it.

Today, it brought a strange moisture to his eyes. But not nearly as much as when he stared down at the beaming face of his soon-to-be wife. And to think, he really did owe this moment to Myone trying to kill him.

Out of evil comes good. Those words were etched on his father's sword. They were Jaden's motto. Caleb had never really understood what they meant. He'd thought it was some pithy saying for humans to make them feel better about their useless, miserable lives. To placate them over the unnecessary suffering the gods laid on them often for no other reason than they were bored.

Now, he knew better. His enemies had meant to kill him. Had been determined to do so. Out of their brutality, he'd found a good that he'd never known existed.

Day follows the night. Nothing lasted forever.

Not the bad.

Not the good.

That thought sobered him as he realized for the first time that Lil was mortal. *He* would live forever.

She wouldn't.

His stomach shrank with something he'd forgotten to think about.

The priest took their arms and wound a decorated ribbon around both their wrists. Caleb paid no attention to the man's words. He was too busy panicking.

What would happen to him once Lil was gone?

"Caleb?"

He blinked at her whisper. "Aye?"

"You didn't answer the priest."

"Sorry. I was overwhelmed by your beauty."

She tsked at him. "Love you, too. But you need to tell our priest that you agree to marry me."

"O-of course! Why else would I be here?"

"You stand here of your own accord?" the priest asked.

"I do. Of course, I do."

With a smile of his own, the priest nodded in approval. "And you, Lilliana?"

"I do."

"Then the gods are pleased. We pray that your union is always a happy one, blessed with many healthy children."

Lilliana was so happy that she was practically dancing by his side.

The priest stepped forward with a bright green cloak that he placed around Lil's shoulders. "May Verlyn protect you and keep you safe."

Then he did the same for Caleb who had to force himself not to balk. He was quite sure his father would protest this if he was here. No doubt, he'd set them all on fire.

But the old priest didn't know, and Caleb didn't want to disillusion him or his misguided belief that Caleb's father was a decent, giving god. Perhaps he was.

After all, Jaden could have killed Myone, or turned her in.

Instead, he protected her and his grandson.

Maybe the old bastard did have a heart.

Or maybe, like him and Xev, his father had changed. Who knew? And the last thing he wanted to think about right then was his father. Lil was the most important thing in the world, and she was what he needed to focus on.

Their future together.

Caleb kissed her lightly on the lips as the door to the temple opened again to the public. People came rushing in with their offerings. Singing and dancing, they placed garland necklaces around Lilliana's neck and his.

Even Xev and Myone received their benedictions.

He had no idea what to make of them. "Why are they so happy?"

Lil smiled at him. "It's solstice. I told you. It marks the new year and new beginnings. They'll have a bonfire later and we'll let go of our past grievances to start anew. That's why I wanted this day for our marriage."

He would never get used to her beautiful spirit and kind heart. Her generosity.

Xev approached him hesitantly. Caleb didn't blame him. They had never been close. Not even friendly, really.

But now Caleb knew something about his brother he hadn't known before.

"You're the double agent who's been giving our intel to the Kalosum." Azura, Noir and Braith would reward Caleb beyond his wildest dreams for that knowledge. They wanted the heart of their betrayer.

And Caleb knew his name.

Xev merely shrugged. "Born of equal parts good and bad. Like you." He took Myone's hand in his and kissed her knuckles. "All it took was a gentle nudge to send me in the right direction." His gaze went to Lilliana. "I imagine you'll be joining me now."

Caleb shook his head. "I'm done with war. I'm a farmer."

"Farmer?" Xev laughed until he realized Caleb meant those words.

Myone held out a small clay pot toward him. "This is why Xev is here. I asked him to bring it for the two of you."

When he didn't take it, she nudged it into his hands. "It's a gift, Malphas. It doesn't bite."

A gift? He'd never expected such a thing, especially not from his brother and the woman who'd tried to kill him.

He had no idea what it was until he lifted the lid.

Honestly, he couldn't have been more shocked to find a cobra in there.

Caleb gaped. "Is this for real?"

Myone nodded. "No one should be separated from the one they love."

No, they shouldn't. And it made him ache for his brother and Myone.

"I can't believe you did this."

"What is it?" Lilliana asked as she frowned at the golden colored blob.

Caleb tilted the jar so that she could see it more clearly. "Your immortality."

"My what?"

"'Tis ambrosia," Caleb explained.

"And nectar." Xev held up a small skin. "The two together will ensure that you never age or die."

"Not completely true." Caleb handed her the jar. "Even immortals can die."

"Like when you were wounded in the cave."

He nodded at Lil. "Exactly. Certain weapons and circumstances can end us."

Her eyes widened. "Circumstances such as what?"

"Beheading," Xev said before Caleb had a chance. "Cutting the head off most things will kill them. Immortal or not."

She rubbed at her neck.

Wanting to reassure her, Caleb nudged it closer to her. "Go ahead, love. Eat it."

Still, she hesitated. "Will it change me?"

"I wouldn't give it to you if it did that. I love you as you are. The last thing I want is for you to change."

A human came near them. "Food?"

"Not for you." Caleb directed the young man toward a group of humans who were sharing honey cakes. Then he turned back to Lil. "You better eat and drink it quick. I'd hate to have to gut one of these fools for stealing your immortality."

She bit her lip. "Is it okay that I do this? The gods won't be angry?"

Xev sucked his breath in between his teeth. "It's rather a gray area. You won't be in trouble. But let's just say if they find out what I've done... well, really, I won't be in any more trouble than I'm normally in. And it'll be significantly less trouble than if they discover I'm not really serving my mother's army. So... eat up before Malphas guts an innocent human."

Laughing, she dipped her fingers into the small clay pot so that she could scoop it out and eat it. "It's delicious."

"Wait until you drink this." Caleb held the skin out to her.

She took a drink, then moaned over the taste. "You're right. Even better."

"Lilli!"

She waved at her father, then handed Caleb the skin. "I'll be right back."

He watched her make her way through the crowd to her father's side.

Myone smiled. "She's sweet. I like her."

"So do I," Xev said.

Caleb smirked at both of them. "As if I care what either of you thinks... but I do owe you. Thank you." He handed the skin to Xev. "I never expected this kindness. Thank you."

Xev sighed. "I know we've had our differences. But I'm glad to see you happy. I wish you a much better ending than the stolen moments we've been forced to share."

Myone nodded. "And I'm glad to have you out of our future battles."

"Given how badly you kicked my ass in the last one, I don't see where that matters."

"It matters." She met Xev's gaze. "I was only able to stab him because he hesitated to harm me."

"Thank you, brother."

Caleb didn't respond. He hated for anyone to know

he held any weakness. He liked to pretend he was as heartless as his parents.

Sadly, he wasn't.

Xev clapped him on the back. "We're going before we draw unwanted attention to our presence, or yours."

Myone didn't let him go so easily. She hugged him. "My best to you and your human."

Then, they were gone.

Caleb felt so alone then. Even though he was in the middle of a huge crowd.

Such a strange feeling actually. It left a deep, hollow sensation in his stomach.

One that didn't vanish until he saw Lil again. He waded his way through the happy celebrants to stand by her side.

"So, how long will all this last?" He gestured at the party.

"'Til dawn."

Her answer stunned him. "I didn't think humans had that kind of stamina."

"Lord of Misrule!"

Caleb scowled at the random shout that filled the air. It was a call that was taken up by others until it became a chant.

A group in the middle of the temple linked hands to form a circle around a man. Chanting, they danced around him while the one they surrounded held his mug up to salute them.

"Human celebrations are so odd."

Lifting up on her toes, she kissed his cheek. "The word you're looking for, husband, is *fun*." She took his hand and pulled him to a space where she could dance with him.

Never had Caleb felt awkward. But this... demons didn't dance. The closest they came to it was battle.

"You're so stiff," Lilliana chided. "Give me your hand and follow my steps."

She made it sound so easy. But he kept stepping on her dainty feet. To his amazement, she didn't care. She just laughed and kept dancing with him.

He would never understand her. How she could be happy over nothing at all.

Her father came up to them with two cups. "Salute to my daughter and new son! May you live long and have many grandchildren for me to love!"

Thanks to his brother and Myone, they would live a long life. And he couldn't wait for it.

As for children... the very thought terrified him. He couldn't imagine being a father.

But then, he could never have imagined being a husband. Or a farmer. Truthfully, he looked forward to being proved wrong about children, too. He only prayed that it was a daughter who was every bit as beautiful as her mother.

Just as he took a drink, several screams sounded from outside.

People came running into the temple.

"Monsters!"

"Hide!"

"Run!"

It seemed like a thousand voices were screaming at once with contradictory orders. The words blurred together. Caleb cut in front of Lilliana to protect her and her father.

Before he could do anything more, a Malachai demon shot fire through the room.

His eyes burned, letting him know they were changing colors. Fangs descended.

Damn it!

He had to get control before he exposed himself to humans who would never understand the difference between him and their enemies.

'Course, he'd been one of those enemies not that long ago, but things had changed.

"Get her hidden," he growled to Ophelos.

"Caleb?"

The note of fear in her voice for him almost brought tears to his eyes. "I'll be fine, mouse. So long as you're unharmed, nothing can touch me." He kissed her quickly, then gently nudged her toward her father. "Hide her."

With a quick nod, her father vanished into the crowd, pulling her behind him.

Caleb hated putting his powers on display, or revealing himself to superstitious humans. But he had no choice. They weren't capable of fighting a Malachai. Even though this demon wasn't their leader, Monakribos, any of the Malachai line was deadly beyond belief.

Caleb let out a piercing whistle. "Hey, asshole! Try someone who isn't afraid of you."

The demon snarled at him, then launched a fireball at him.

Caleb caught it. He held it in his hand, then levitated it above his palm. "That's the way you want this, huh?"

"What are you?"

"Son of Verlyn." While Caleb hated invoking his father's name, this was the only time that truly warranted it.

Shock flitted across the demon's face. "You lie!"

He launched the fireball back at him. Then created another and sent it quickly behind the first.

His shot landed square in the demon's chest. He cried out in pain, then hissed and launched himself at Caleb.

Caleb caught him and kneed him in the gut.

"I will kill you!" the demon snarled.

"Not the first to say that. Guarantee you're not the last." Caleb shoved him back.

The demon caught him with a vicious punch to his chin that was staggering. But the pain invigorated him. It was a mother's caress. All he'd known in his life was brutality.

Blood.

Death.

Growling, he let his claws spring out. He slashed at the demon, then head butted him.

The demon pulled a knife and tried to stab Caleb in the neck. He caught his hand and twisted the knife out of his grasp. The demon answered by dragging his claws across Caleb's back.

Angry at himself for being so stupid, he conjured his armor.

The demon gasped as recognition darkened his eyes.

Aye, that was a stupid move. Caleb had given no thought to the fact that he was a commander of the army this demon fought in. Any of their soldiers would know his emblem.

But it was too late now. He'd outed himself.

"Fighting for the human wretches?"

"Better than fighting for continued captivity. What

do you think Monakribos will do to you once this war is over? Never mind the gods you serve."

"I will be rewarded!"

"You'll be killed, captured or enslaved." It was what was always done to them— and that was from the dark lords they served. They were only allowed freedom when there was war. It was why Caleb had fought so hard against the Kalosum. The longer the war went on, the less he had to worry about the dark ones leashing his powers and his freedom.

Honestly, they'd be better off if the Kalosum won. They might actually show mercy on them. The Mavromino would rip them apart even in victory. They only existed to abuse and subjugate their ilk.

The Malachai demon rushed at him, then took flight.

No, you don't.

Caleb blasted him with everything he had, knowing if he returned to their gods, he would tell them that Caleb had defected. That was the last thing he wanted.

The Malachai hit the ground with an echoing scream that didn't fade until the pathetic creature was nothing more than ash on the ground.

Only then did the humans slowly emerge from hiding. One by one, they returned to the main floor.

Caleb tensed as he waited for them to attack him.

The priest was the first one to come near. "You saved us, my lord. You really are the son of Verlyn."

Wait... what?

Part of him wanted to hiss and shrink away from them. He really expected them to attack. Why weren't they attacking?

Suddenly, Lil was by his side. "It's all right, Caleb." She rubbed his back comfortingly.

Still, he wanted to run away. A crowd surrounding him had never boded well for him or any demon he knew.

But they weren't attacking. They were offering gratitude. Some were offering drink.

Was this real? It seemed like a dream.

"Don't leave me," he whispered to her.

Lilliana tightened her grip on his hand. "They love you, Caleb. Enjoy the moment."

Still, he wanted to run. Especially when the villagers came up to him to thank him personally for doing what he did by nature— kill a demon or anything else that got in his way.

It was several minutes before he finally relaxed and began to accept the fact that they meant him no harm.

"You're a hero, husband. And not just to me."

A hero. The thought wrenched his gut. He wasn't

meant to be a hero. And that title was ill-fitting to the demonic part of himself that he took pride in.

His father would vomit if he heard that. Or the cheers that rang out to celebrate a son Jaden had thrown away.

Someone handed him a cup of mead. "Well done!"

"It would have been better done if I wasn't covered in blood."

The unknown man laughed as he vanished in the crowd.

Then, the man they'd declared as the Lord of Misrule stepped forward and offered Caleb his motley, belled hat. "I take my hat off to you, sir, and declare you the real Lord of Misrule for the year."

That caused a cheer to rise up from the others.

Scowling, he turned toward Lil. "What does this mean?"

"You get to spend the rest of the night playing pranks on others."

"I don't know how to do that."

"I know, precious. But smile. It's a good thing."

He still wasn't so sure about that. But with her, there was no such thing as bad. Neither in her attitude nor reality. Her presence made everything better.

And as the night passed without another incident, he slowly began to relax.

Her father came up and clapped him on the back. "Well, this has been the tamest Lord of Misrule we've ever had. I think the people are actually grateful for that after the demon mishap." He smiled at Caleb. "But I'm sure you're ready for your wedding night."

Lil blushed profusely.

Clearing his throat, her father stepped back. "You two can have the cottage to yourselves. I'll stay in the village and continue to celebrate."

"Thank you, Papa." She kissed his cheek.

It wasn't until they started home that Caleb understood the full gift her father was giving them.

Lilliana hugged him close. "I hope we conceive a child tonight. I can think of no better gift than a little Caleb."

4

ONE YEAR LATER

"What do you think?"

Caleb smiled at the pride on Ophelos's face. Refusing any help from anyone, the old man had spent month after month building this addition onto their cottage.

A private room for Caleb and Lil, along with a special alcove for a crib even though Lil had yet to conceive.

Her father had thought of everything.

"I think it's perfect." Caleb looked at Lil who had tears in her eyes.

"Thank you, Papa. I love it!"

Smiling, her father left them alone to inspect their new accommodations.

"There's only one thing missing."

She arched a brow at him. "What?"

Caleb manifested his sword.

She gasped. "I didn't know you still had that."

"I can't let it go. If it fell into the hands of an enemy, they could use it to enslave me."

"Can you not destroy it?"

He shook his head. "Forged by gods for gods. It's even more immortal than I am. All I can do is hide it away."

Making sure it was wrapped in his enchanted cloak that kept it hidden from anyone who might try to track him with it, he used his powers to carefully conceal his sword in the wall, over their bed.

Lil leaned against him. "I pray that you never again reach for this sword, Lord Husband. But should the day ever come when you must return to war, then it should be to protect what you love. Never again for hatred or fear. And never should you battle for vengeance."

Love, gratitude, and hope mixed inside him. He loved the way she viewed the world. Most of all, he loved her heart.

"I will *never* touch it again. You're my home, Lil. For all eternity. And here I'll remain until the world ends."

She smiled up at him. "And hopefully we'll fill this cottage with beautiful children."

That was their hope. And yet Caleb couldn't shake

the feeling that this couldn't last. His past was too brutal. Too harsh.

He still couldn't believe none of his soldiers had come calling for him. Surely, they'd been looking. He hoped that Xev had helped to deflect them from their search. But he had no way of knowing for sure. He hadn't seen or heard from his brother since their wedding a year ago.

"You know what tonight is?"

Caleb hid his smile and feigned confusion. "Middle of the week."

"Well... yes. But..." She paused expectantly.

"I forgot a chore?"

"You really don't remember?"

Caleb screwed his face up. "We need to herd the sheep?"

"Are you serious?"

Laughing, he picked her up. "I seem to recall marrying a certain little mouse on this day a year ago."

"You did remember!"

"How could I forget the first day of my life? The best day of my existence."

She hugged his neck, then kissed his cheek. "Love you."

"Love you more." And he meant that. There was nothing he wouldn't do for her.

That thought was foremost on his mind later that night when they entered the village where everyone was out in celebration. This time, he didn't mind the crowd. He even sampled some of the vendor foods. Mostly because he enjoyed watching Lil try them.

If she liked it, her blue eyes widened, and she ate more. If she didn't care for it, she'd wrinkle her nose and shake her head. He found both reactions adorable.

And he was laughing at her enjoyment when he felt a presence behind him.

Xev.

There was no mistaking the ripple of power that emanated from his brother. It raised the hair on the back of his arms and caused his patience to dissolve.

He turned around abruptly to confront him. "What?"

Xev arched a brow. "No greeting?"

"Glad to see my favorite hemorrhoid. Why are you here?"

"Meeting Myone. But I also wanted to see you."

"Why?"

Xev snorted. "You just won't let that go, will you?"

In spite of Xev's kindness a year ago, it didn't undo a lifetime of their ill will toward each other. "I know you, brother. Which means I trust you not at all. And I know you're not here for no reason."

"Xev!" Lil drew him into a hug that irritated Caleb even more.

He knew there was nothing behind her hug, but still... he didn't want to even share her hugs with her father. Never mind a brother he'd spent more of his life fighting than getting along with.

"Did you come to celebrate with us?"

Caleb gave him a smirk. "Yeah, brother. Did you come to celebrate with us?"

"I would love to, but I need to speak with Caleb first... if you don't mind?"

Worry creased her brow. "Is everything all right?"

"Just a message from our father. I'm sure he'll tell you about it later."

Xev motioned for Caleb to follow him away from Lil and the crowd.

Caleb growled low in his throat as he treaded after him. Although, he had a sudden urge to blast Xev. Wouldn't hurt him any, but it might make Caleb feel better.

Once they were alone, Xev let out a tired breath. "You have no idea what's going on, do you?"

"I know you're annoying me. Is there anything else I should be focusing on?"

"The war. Lyseah has claimed your army and is—"

"I don't care."

A tic started in Xev's cheek. "They are attacking humans."

"They're not attacking here."

"What if they do?"

Caleb gave him a hate-filled glare. "They'll seriously regret it."

"We could use your help."

Caleb laughed. "Have you lost your mind? I can't just go back and pretend nothing happened. Have you met your mother? Our uncle or aunt? They're not trusting gods. They'll gut me if I show up after all this time."

"Myone could take you to our father."

Caleb smirked in disbelief. "I know you didn't just suggest that. And why aren't you fighting with the Kols?"

Xev looked away sheepishly. Because he knew what Caleb did. They were turncoats. Didn't matter who they killed, what they believed or what they did. They were both born half evil. No one on their father's side would ever accept them as anything other than traitors and liars.

"Exactly, Xev. There's no going back. I knew that when I decided to stay and honestly, I'm good with that." Caleb started away, then stopped himself. "How's your son?"

"Healthy. Beautiful. His name's Jared."

"Who named him?"

A slight smile played at the edges of Xev's lips. "Myone."

Caleb nodded. "I hope he grows up happy."

"Thank you. I hope war and trouble never find you."

Inclining his head to his brother, Caleb made his way back into the crowd to find Lilliana.

"Where's your brother?"

"He had things he had to attend to."

She frowned. "He's not staying?"

"No. But he wishes us well."

Lil looked past his shoulders as if seeking Xev in the crowd. "What was so imperative?"

"He was giving me news of our father and of the war."

Fear darkened her eyes. "Is it bad?"

"Not at all." Kissing her forehead, he savored this moment with her. "We're going to be fine. Trust me." But even as he said those words, he wondered how long they'd last.

As much as he wanted to deny it, he knew Xev was right. If the gods didn't kill each other off, it was just a matter of time before their war spilled over this world.

I hope you all kill each other off. That would be the best outcome.

But gods didn't die easily. Demons even less so.

Sighing, he tried to put it out of his mind and focus on the celebration Lil loved so much.

Caleb wiped the sweat from his brow as he weeded the garden near their cottage. Sitting back on his haunches, he still couldn't believe he was here.

Doing this.

Some would see this as a downfall, but he'd never been happier. Every day he woke up beside Lil was a miracle. Her eyes still glowed with warmth and love whenever she looked at him. He'd never understand that. He was only grateful to have her.

Funny how he could still see that day all those years ago when her father had built them a room on to their cottage.

Their own private room with an area for a nursery.

While they still didn't have that child they craved, he

was more than content. He tried to tell himself that it was for the best. Surely, he wasn't father material.

But Lil would be an incredible mother. He hated that she had yet to fulfill the role she craved.

We have time. Eternity, actually.

The baby would come when he or she was meant to. There was no need to worry about it.

He glanced to the cottage where Lil was baking. Then, he looked back at their garden. He really needed to finish weeding.

Screw it, the weeds weren't going anywhere. He wanted to see his wife.

Rising to his feet, he headed for the door. But he'd barely reached the halfway point when he heard someone rushing toward him on horseback. Since they seldom had visitors, and never unexpected ones, Caleb ran to the door so that he could put himself between the rider and Lil.

As the rider skidded to a stop, he recognized him from the village.

"We're under attack! We need every man capable of holding a sword or club." He didn't wait for Caleb to speak before he rode off again.

"Caleb?" Lil came running up to him.

He caught her against his side. "Don't worry. I won't leave you."

She drew a ragged breath. "They'll need you. None of them are trained."

"I don't care. Let them fight it out."

"They're our friends, Caleb. We can't let them die."

Of course, they could. It really wasn't that hard. Just stand back and do nothing. People and demons did that every day.

But he couldn't do that to her. She trembled against him, and her eyes shone with unshed tears.

"Fine. But I'm taking you to our cave so that you can hide until this is over. Grab what you need and prepare to stay there for a few days."

"Very well. Thank you."

"Don't thank me for being stupid. Just pray we don't regret this."

Against his better judgment, he went to the bedroom and did what he'd sworn he'd never do. He removed his sword from the wall.

Maybe this'll be enough.

If he went to war with this sword, any demonic army would know him. Maybe that would scare them off.

Or antagonize them more. He had no idea what kind of bounty would be on his head. He'd deserted his post. There was no way his masters would forgive him for that. After all, they weren't known for forgiveness.

Gutting enemies and allies, definitely.

But never giving anyone a pass.

Irritated that this was happening, Caleb summoned his armor.

A gasp sounded from behind him. He turned to find Lil in the doorway. "What's wrong?"

She smiled a smile that made his stomach tighten. "I forgot how scary you are in your armor... and how handsome."

"I forgot how heavy it was." He rolled his shoulders.

"Can you still take your demonic form?"

Caleb hesitated. Could he? It'd been so long that he wasn't sure. "I don't know." Closing his eyes, he focused inward.

"Yes... yes you can."

He opened his eyes to see his blood red skin. Laughing, he tsked at her. "You fell in love with me looking like this."

"True. You're beautiful to me in either form. But my fear is that our friends won't be as understanding if they see your demon skin."

"Probably not and while I like to scare the natives shaking their pitchforks, I don't want to have to hurt one of them. Especially not one we've had over for dinner."

"Then I suggest a more human appearance."

"Mmm." He switched back to his birth form. Strange

how this hated body had become comfortable. Thanks to her.

Everything he had was thanks to Lil. It was why he couldn't afford for anything bad to happen. If he lost her, he had no idea what would become of him.

And he didn't want to find out.

So he took her to their cave and made a fire for her with his powers. Then, he pulled her into his arms.

"You're holding me too tightly."

"I know. I just don't want to let you go."

"I'll be right here, Caleb. No one will come to our cave. I'm safe."

"You better be."

"I will and you better stay safe."

Caleb scoffed. "I'm too mean to die."

"Good. Now go quickly so that you can get back to me."

He kissed her, savoring the taste of her lips. Until she gently pushed him back.

"All right, bossy. I'm going." But as he left, a bad feeling came over him.

He didn't want to be gone long. Spreading his wings, he flew to the village where they'd married.

Yet he didn't have to go far before he saw the smoke and smelled the stench of death. Gods, how could he have ever forgotten that smell? It was rancid and stuck in his throat.

How could he have lived for this?

I was an idiot.

A part of him wanted to return to Lil and fly her far away from this hell hole. But he knew she'd never willingly leave. It wasn't in her.

No. She was a woman of convictions. A woman of decency.

He owed her everything.

"Malphas?"

He cursed as he recognized Itzal's voice. Of course, his brother would be here. "Itzal."

"It is you! Where have you been? I thought you were dead. We all did."

"Not dead. Any chance I can talk you out of this attack?"

"What?"

Caleb grimaced at the carnage. The humans had been ill prepared for the demon horde. "Pull back. Why are you going after children? What's the point?"

"They are the pets that our enemies favor. Azura wants them wiped from the planet."

Of course, she did. She was petty and vicious that way.

"Itzal... pull back your forces."

"What? Why?"

"Pull them back. Otherwise, we'll be enemies."

Itzal laughed. Until he realized Caleb was serious. "You're on their side?"

"Looks like." He unsheathed his sword. "I don't want to hurt you, brother. Please don't make me do something I'd rather not."

"Don't make me kill you, Malphas."

"Then we're at war." He started toward Itzal who quickly flew away.

That changed nothing. Other than the fact that Caleb was about to fly into a mess.

The moment he joined the fray, the Sephirii attacked him.

Of course, they did. Once a demon, always a demon.

Unwilling to harm them, he took their blows as he tried to go after his brethren.

"Stop!"

He froze along with those around him as he heard Myone shout.

"Caleb is fighting for *us*. Do not harm him."

Those words resonated in his ears as he realized exactly what he'd just done.

And that Myone had stood up for him. Vouched for him. Incredible. Honestly, he couldn't believe it. Only Lil had ever done that for him.

Then, Caleb's gaze went to the red-headed young warrior next to her.

Jared. He could feel the pull of Xev's power inside the boy's heart. Lean, yet ripped, he was a lethal warrior already. Once he grew more into his powers...

He'd be invincible.

Without thinking, Caleb saluted his nephew with his sword.

Jared frowned, then returned to fighting the demons. The kid would have no idea who he was. And that was fine. At least he was able to see him.

Caleb returned to the battle. This time with allies. And though it wasn't easy, they did eventually route the demons.

Itzal survived, though to be honest, he wasn't sure if that was a good idea or not. No doubt, he'd be the first to tell Azura of Caleb's defection.

There was nothing to be done for it now. The humans were safe. He was bloody and there were bodies everywhere.

For the first time, he actually felt something for the lost lives. He knew most of them. Had laughed with them.

Celebrated solstice and other holidays with them and their families.

Now, they were gone. The pain in his heart was searing. A demon who cared about human lives. It was prophetic and painful. In that moment, he realized just how much Lil had changed him.

Not for the better.

He missed not caring. Being completely numb to death. More to the point, praying for death every time he went into battle. Anything to make him feel something.

Then, he'd found Lil. He still couldn't believe how lucky he'd been.

Needing to see her, he flew off to their cave that seemed to be much farther away than it was when he'd dropped her there. Interminable, point of fact.

Worse, it was quieter.

Darker. There was no light whatsoever. And that made his gut clench tight.

"Lil?"

No answer.

Unbelievable terror filled him. A million horrific images went through his mind. The worst ones showed her lying on the ground, like the horror he'd just left on the battlefield.

"Lil?" His voice cracked, and his legs almost buckled as he searched the darkness for some sign of her.

Where could she be?

Suddenly, he saw a flickering light coming toward

him. His nostrils flaring, he went to confront whoever had harmed his wife. He was going to rip them...

That thought scattered as he saw the tiny, slight form of his wife. "Lil!"

Lilliana was completely unprepared for the ferocity of Caleb's hug. She was used to him holding her close and tight. But this...

"Are you all right?"

He trembled in her arms. "I thought you were... I can't even say the words."

"I'm right here, love. I'm not going anywhere."

Still, he held on to her. "You cannot die, Lil. No harm can ever come to you. Do you understand?"

She wanted to call him silly. Of course, she wasn't going anywhere. She was immortal. But this didn't seem like the time to point it out. So, she decided to change the subject. "Did we win?"

"No."

Tears filled her eyes. "What?"

With a ragged sigh, he stepped back from her and cupped her face in his hands. "I mean yes. Technically, we won. They've been routed. But no one ever wins a war. A lot of the villagers died. I'm sorry."

Her heart broke for the families who would be torn apart. For the lives that were gone. It was so unfair.

"I still have you. That's enough. Thank you for helping them."

Caleb offered her a smile as he finally stepped away. He tucked his wings into his back. "I think we should stay here."

She was aghast at his words. "I didn't bring enough supplies."

"I can gather what we need. The farm's too big a risk for us now."

She wanted to argue, but the expression on his face stilled her tongue. He wasn't about to listen. Not right now. He was too upset.

Better to humor him. She could make her case for returning home after he calmed down.

How she wished her father was still alive. He'd know how to talk sense into her husband. For some reason, Caleb had often deferred to her father.

Then again, she was glad her father wasn't here to witness this nightmare. The loss of his friends.

It would break his heart.

Caleb swallowed hard. "I will keep you safe, Lil. I promise."

∾

AZURA GLARED at the demon in front of her. "Repeat what you just told me."

"Malphas was fighting with the Kalosum."

Those words brought a level of fury to her she wouldn't have thought possible. Which given the state of fury she normally lived in said a lot.

That anger vibrated through her body, making her limbs shake. Unable to stand it, she blasted the demon in front of her.

"Killing messengers again, are we?" her brother asked as he came into the room where she was pacing.

"Shut up, Noir. I've no time for you. And even less patience."

He toed at the dust on the floor that used to be an almost competent demon. "I see. May I ask what has set you on fire?"

"We've lost Malphas."

"How careless of someone. Any idea where they last put him?"

She glared at the arrogant ass. Always so pompous ... and galling. "You're not funny."

"I'm hilarious. You've just never fully appreciated me."

She scoffed. "Either find something useful to say or go find a demon to flay."

He considered that. "I do like flaying demons.

They're quite entertaining when they beg for their lives."

She let out a long-suffering sigh. "Fine then, since you're looking for something to torture, bring me the heart and/or head of Malphas!"

He arched a brow at that. "You know he's a son of Verlyn, right?"

"Since when does Verlyn care about his children?"

"Probably as much as we care about our daughter. However, if one of our siblings attacked her, I do believe we'd be demanding a proper gutting from them."

"Why are you being reasonable? Isn't that against your nature?"

Noir quirked an irritating grin. "Self-preservation is always my priority. But while you're contemplating his death and dismemberment, have you considered something?"

"What?"

"Why the defection?"

Azura paused at the obvious question that had yet to occur to her. "You may have a point."

"Of course, I do. And unlike you, I'm not over-reacting."

Those words irritated her. As if he wasn't known for throwing his own tantrums. Most of them far bloodier than anything she'd ever conceived.

Noir approached her purposefully. "Think about it. You have one of our most vicious soldiers who suddenly stops fighting. Then, he shows up years later on the side of our enemies. What does that sound like to you?"

"Stupid?"

He rolled his eyes at her. "Sounds like ... love," he sneered the word. "Obviously, someone tamed our favorite animal. We just need to find out who."

"Then destroy them."

"Exactly."

6

Caleb sighed as he followed Lil from the bedroom into the kitchen. "Please listen to me, Lil. I think it's a bad idea. Let's stay home tonight."

"It's solstice. You know how important this is to me."

"The war's getting worse."

"Then they'll need protection and you'll be there to help again if there's any trouble."

Caleb growled in frustration. Why was she being so impossible? "Please, Lil. I have a bad feeling."

She paused to give him a sweet smile. "You always have bad feelings. Why is this different?"

Because it was. His gut was knotted, and he couldn't explain it. But he understood her point. He'd had misgivings in the past and had acted on them.

And been wrong.

This was different. It was as if every part of his being screamed out in protest. "I really think we should stay home."

"Caleb... don't."

And that finished that. As much as he wanted to argue, he knew it was useless. She owned him. Lock, stock, and barrel.

He could deny her nothing. As much as he wanted to put her in a closet and keep her away from the world, he could never hurt her. Not even her feelings. He'd rather be gutted than harm her in any way.

So when she put her foot down, he had no choice other than to cave.

Damn it.

At least he knew Myone and Xev would be there. He could rely on them to help guard the only thing that mattered in his life.

Please don't let me regret this.

He wouldn't be able to forgive himself if anything happened to her because he failed to protect her.

So, he prepared for a celebration he really didn't want to attend. And tried to focus on the fact that it made her happy and the last thing he wanted to do was dull her smile in any way.

They waited until the sun had fallen before they

made their way to the village. Strange how this place had become home. There had been a time, not that long ago when he would have burned this place to the ground and not cared.

Humans...

They were his friends now. He glanced to Lilliana. His family.

He'd never get used to that. She ran off into the crowd. Caleb started after her, only to find Xev in his way.

"Do you mind?"

Xev grinned. "Never. It's one of my more irritating qualities."

"Yes, it is. Out of my way, idiot."

"She's fine. Myone's keeping an eye on Lil."

That made him feel a little better. "We have to stop these talks. Every time I see you, my sphincter clenches. Can't you ever just say nice weather? How are the crops growing?"

"How do you know I wasn't planning on asking that?"

"Were you?"

That annoying grin returned to Xev's face. "No. But you shouldn't jump to conclusions."

"I hate you so much."

"I know. But you need to put that aside. My mother knows that you have a weakness."

Those words tore through him like glass. "What do you mean?"

"It didn't take much for her and the King of All Darkness to figure out why you vanished and then showed up on the wrong side."

Caleb cursed his stupidity. He'd betrayed himself.

For Lil.

"Do they know who she is?"

"Not as far as I know." Xev sighed. "But let's face it, I'm not my mother's confidante. She thinks you and I are still fighting, and not talking. That gives you an advantage."

Maybe. He still wasn't sure. And he definitely didn't want to be wrong. Not about this.

Not about them.

They were the ultimate evil. And there was no stopping them from their cruelty. Xev was a perfect example. Azura had no mercy for her own child. She'd throw him to their enemies even faster than she'd betray Caleb. Nothing mattered to her other than power.

No, that wasn't true. She wanted to kill her "good" siblings more than she wanted to do anything else. That was what drove her. Azura wanted to punish the ones who held her back.

Punish anyone who got in her way.

Right now, Caleb shared that last sentiment. He was more than willing to sacrifice her for the sake of his sanity.

"You have any other good news to tell me?"

"My boy's now commanding his own legion."

Caleb arched a brow, especially at the proud tone in his brother's voice. "I have no response to that. Though I feel like you're looking for a congratulations."

"Little bit. Could you sound more insincere?"

"Not sure I should be happy he's helping kill my kind."

Xev looked around the crowd that surrounded them. "You sure they're still your kind? It looks to me like you've upgraded."

Caleb wanted to argue. But honestly, Xev was right. If he'd learned nothing else while living with his wife, it was that people had hearts. They weren't the insignificant animals he'd once thought them to be.

Humans were special and he was lucky to have found the most remarkable one of all. He was even luckier that she loved him back.

And that made his gut tighten again. "Xev... may I ask you a favor?"

His jaw went slack. "You're asking me for another

favor? There must be sun shining in Azmodea right now."

"Not funny."

"Not trying to be. Just amazed by your audacity."

And they were words Caleb had never thought he'd utter. Asking for help was hard enough.

Asking for a favor...

It wasn't in him.

Or so he'd thought.

Apparently, he really would do anything for her. "I need you to help me protect Lil."

"You know I will, especially after everything you've done for me and Myone... and Jared. I owe you."

"Don't forget it." Caleb left so that he could find Lilliana.

She was in a group of her friends, drinking mead, and laughing. Caleb paused to take the moment in. To savor this moment of her happiness and beauty. If he could, he'd make this night last forever.

That was his thought until he saw a shadow on his left. Frowning, Caleb made his way over to it.

But there was nothing there.

I'm seeing things.

If it were any night other than solstice, he might actually believe that. Tonight, however, the veil was thin. Things could cross over.

And they would be more powerful than normal.

"Here, kitty, kitty, kitty." He searched the darkness, trying his best to locate what he'd seen.

A bad feeling washed over him.

What was going on?

"Here, demon, demon, demon." The voice whispered on the wind, mocking his earlier call.

Caleb turned around. All he saw was humans, innocent humans, celebrating. "Where are you?"

"We're everywhere." It was right in his ear.

But no one was there.

Screw it! Furious, he ran back to where he'd last seen Lil. All that mattered was keeping her safe.

As he ran, he didn't see the revelers or friends. He saw targets. If they got between him and his wife, he'd annihilate them.

"Lil?" he called out for her.

No one answered.

"Lil!"

"She's right here."

He turned at the sound of Myone's voice. Both of them were staring at him as if he were mad.

Not caring what anyone thought, he pulled his wife against his chest and thanked the gods that she was all right. That the shadow hadn't gone near her.

"Caleb?"

He couldn't respond. His heart was in his throat, choking him with the weight of his relief. "There's something here. Something from the Mavromino. I saw it."

Myone began looking around. "Xev!" she called out to him through the crowd.

Xev appeared by her side instantly. "What's wrong?"

"We have an enemy in our midst. Help me find them."

Xev inclined his head before he stepped back and vanished.

Myone sighed as she looked at him and Lil. "I assume Xev told you the news?"

"That our enemies know how to break me? Yes."

Myone winced. "Then we need to secure you both."

Caleb started laughing. Until he realized it wasn't a joke. "You want to take me to Katoteros? Are you out of your mind?"

"You have a better idea?" she asked.

"Start pulling off my body parts and feeding them to me?"

Lil scowled at them. "What are you talking about? What's Katoteros?"

"The realm where our kind lives. We'll be able to protect you there."

Lil blinked twice. "Leave my home?"

"You have no choice." Myone jerked her chin toward

Caleb. "Neither of you can stay here after this. They'll come for you."

Lil let out a tired sigh as she faced Caleb. "I'm sorry."

"For what?"

"Telling you to take out your sword. This is all my fault."

He pulled her against him. "No, precious. It's not. They would have found me eventually."

"Caleb's right. They would have."

With a ragged breath, she nodded. "I shall miss our cottage. But as long as I'm with you, everything's fine."

Caleb was so grateful she was being reasonable. Though he was surprised. She loved her home, and he hated taking her from it. "We'll be back here. I promise."

She smiled. "I plan to hold you to that."

A YEAR *later*

"WHERE'S CALEB?" Xev asked his son, breathless from the strain of trying to get to his brother.

Jared frowned at him. "He left with his army."

Xev winced. "Your mother's with him?"

"Of course."

Damn it. He was too late. "It's a trap. They lured Caleb and your mother out of here."

Jared paled. "What?"

"I just found out about their plan. The Mavromino lured them out on purpose. They're coming. We have to secure the children and women. They'll hit us where we're weakest. You stay here in case they break through. I have to get to Lil and warn her. She'll be their first target. If they reach her, they can neutralize Caleb's forces and crash the gates."

"Stay here? I can't do that, uncle."

Xev wanted to correct him on that fact. But this wasn't the time or place. He had to get to Lil.

"Send a messenger to Caleb and Myone. Let them know. I'll take some men and hold them off as best I can."

Jared inclined his head. "Good luck."

They'd need more than that. They were going to need a miracle.

"MALPHAS!"

Caleb paused in his attack as he heard his name called. He saw one of the Sephirii heading toward him.

By the speed and expression on his face, Caleb could tell something was wrong.

It made his heart sink. "What's wrong?"

But then he knew. There would only be one reason for someone to come after him while in battle. More than that, he could feel it with every fiber of his being.

Lil was in danger.

Ignoring the battle, he sped home as fast as he could.

The instant he arrived, he smelled the stench of burning flesh. Heard the screams of victims.

Saw the smoke and carnage.

No! His soul screamed out in denial. But there was no denial of this. Everywhere he looked, there was blood and mangled bodies.

"Lil!" he screamed, searching among the victims.

All he heard were whimpers and those begging for help. Tears filled his eyes. He had to find her. "Don't be dead." She couldn't be.

As fast as he could, he made his way to their home.

Lil wasn't there. Caleb staggered in relief. He would find her. She'd be fine.

She would.

"Lilliana! Where are you?"

Still, nothing.

His anger began to build. Why would she not

answer him? Was she still angry that he'd flown to battle? If she was, this was no way to punish him.

"I swear Lil..." He broke off as his foot brushed up against something soft.

Caleb looked down and his entire world came undone.

No... no... It was the only word that he could think or say.

Not Lil. Anyone but Lil.

Dropping to his knees, he gathered her body up in his arms and cried out in anguish. He cupped her face in his hands and sobbed.

How could she be gone? How?

Why was he still alive? He had no reason to live without her.

All he knew was that he was going to rain hell down on all those who had a hand in this. No one would be spared. No one would have mercy.

If it took him a million lifetimes, he would destroy them all.

Caleb still wasn't sure how he'd let Ambrose and crew talk him into this. He hated Christmas and anything to do with this time of year.

Solstice ...

It could all burn for what he cared.

Xev should remember why. Yet he'd been instrumental in forcing Caleb to attend their stupid holiday at the bar and grill, Sanctuary, that was owned by a family of shape shifters.

I am out of my mind.

Only a fool would agree to this. Yet here he was, half a block away, staring at the building. Holiday music filled his ears as the Howlers sang carols. It was a wonder the humans weren't complaining about the noise. But then, they were talented. The music actually calmed him.

Even though it reminded him of the revelers from centuries ago. An image of Lil laughing taunted him. She would love this ...

He started to turn around, then stopped himself. He'd made a promise. The least he could do was fulfill it.

"I hate myself."

Right now, he was hating his brother more.

You might as well get this over with.

Stop in. Say hi. Leave.

He could do that.

Steeling himself, he crossed the street and went to the door where Remi Peltier stood guard. The huge, blond werebear was actually wearing a Santa hat.

"Did you lose a bet?"

Remi snorted. "Close. My wife made me. She said I looked ... *cute.*"

Caleb would mock that, but it hit a little too close to home, so he made no comment. He merely grunted and walked inside.

Wow. He had to give the bears and wolves credit. The place looked as if the North Pole had exploded. Aimee Peltier came up to him with a cup of... he had no idea. It was yellow, hot and frothy.

"Glad you're here, Caleb." She kissed his cheek and handed him a cup.

"What is this?"

"Eggnog. Have some. It's delicious," her daughter said as she joined them and held out a platter of cookies toward him.

"Thanks, Nikki." He took one that was a blue mitten.

"You're welcome." Nikki pranced off in the same direction her mother had vanished.

Caleb bit into the sugar cookie first, then tried the eggnog. Yeah, okay, it wasn't disgusting. Wasn't delicious, but it was tolerable.

"Uncle Cay-Cay!"

He smiled as Xev's daughter ran over to give him a hug. "Hey, sweetie."

"Thank you for coming! I just won a bet with Ambrose. Hah! I'm going shopping tomorrow!"

"Of course, you did." Leave it to Ambrose to bet on whether or not he'd be here. But it was okay. In spite of his ire over being wrangled into this he was enjoying it more than he'd ever admit.

"Hey, Caleb." Acheron patted him on the back as he came over to him. "Can't believe you made it."

He didn't respond to that. "Where are your kids?"

Acheron jerked his chin toward the stage. "Singing with the Howlers and their mom."

A beautiful brunette woman around the age of twenty-four came up and placed a baby boy dressed as an elf in Acheron's arms. It took Caleb a moment to realize this was Ash's granddaughter Artemisia with her latest son. "Could you hold him a minute, Papa? I have to go change."

It was only then that Caleb realized the baby had spit up all the way down her back.

Ash took the infant and laughed. He snapped his fingers and Artemisia's clothes were clean. "I'll keep the baby. Feel free to mingle."

She kissed his cheek. "Thank you. Love you!"

"Love you more."

Caleb suddenly felt out of place. Everywhere he looked, his friends were gathered. Ambrose, Nyria, their children. Fang. Vane. Zarek and Astrid. Valerius and Tabitha with their kids and grandkids. Even Sasha was here with his wife and kids. Urian. Sarraxyn. The list seemed endless.

He knew their joy. He'd felt it so long ago.

No, he still felt it now. Even after all this time, Lil was with him. She continued to live in his heart.

My greatest treasure.

My greatest pain.

He'd known real love and the absence of it burned deep in his soul. Nothing soothed it, and events like this only served to remind him how hard it was.

How much he'd lost.

Why am I still alive?

Obviously, the answer was to suffer.

"Why aren't you with your brother?"

Caleb turned his gaze toward Styxx who was Ash's twin. He was on the other side of the room with his wife and herd. "Notice you're not standing next to your brother."

Ash laughed. "I was until I saw you, and I will be again before the end of the night."

"If you say so." But Caleb knew that in spite of their pasts, Styxx and Ash were best friends. Just as he'd forgiven Xev for letting Lil die.

Not an easy thing to forgive. But carrying a grudge was pointless.

"Why you so sad, akri-Caleb?"

He smiled as Ash's demon daughter, Simi, joined him and Acheron. Dressed in a short Santa dress with bells hanging from her red horns, she was as adorable as her daughter was.

"I'm not sad, Sim."

She tsked at him. "The Simi feels it in your heart. You carry sadness even though you're smiling."

He would deny it, but the Charonte could easily see inside him. "I'm fine, Simi."

But really, she was right. There was a deep sadness inside that continued to burn. It was hard to be the only one present who had never found someone.

I'm the weird uncle who gets to sit at the kids' table.

Part of a family, but eternally alone.

Yeah. Yesterday, demon warrior feared by all. Today, the one they all pitied.

Whoever had said it was better to have loved and lost than to have never loved at all was an idiot who'd never loved anyone. If he had, then he would have known that time didn't heal all wounds. And that some pains never went away. They didn't even really numb.

They just hurt, not matter what.

He should have stayed home.

Suddenly, bells rang out. Along with a loud thud against the roof.

He would have thought they were under attack, but everyone else seemed to think it was normal.

Since this was the first one of these parties he'd ever attended, maybe it was.

"Ho ho ho!"

Caleb groaned as Julian of Macedon came into the room, dressed as Santa. Complete with red suit, beard and a huge sack of presents.

"What on earth?" Caleb asked.

Ash laughed. "He drew the short straw last year. You should have been here when Kyrian and Talon were Santa."

Simi snorted loudly. "The Simi's favorite was the year Bethany was Santa."

Acheron nodded. "Oh yeah. That was a particularly interesting costume that year."

"And alls them little kids gots swords that year," Simi said.

Caleb could just imagine. After Lil's death, Bethany had been his boss for a while. She was all about fair play ...

And battle.

But to be honest, he enjoyed watching the kids run up to Julian to get a gift. There was so much happiness that he was glad he'd fought on the right side.

This ... this needed preserving.

Even though right now it seemed like evil might actually win, and that the world today was almost as scary as his past, there was hope.

There was still kindness and love.

For the world, not so much for himself.

Sighing, he watched as Acheron took his great-grandson up to Julian to receive a present. Of course,

Simi went, too, to make sure the baby got a bottle of barbecue sauce.

His heart happy and aching, Caleb decided they didn't really need him here.

But as he started to leave, someone grabbed his arm.

On instinct, he almost punched the culprit. Until he saw Xev there, along with Aeron, Vawn, Kaziel and Ambrose.

"You leaving?" Ambrose asked.

"I said I'd come, and I came. Didn't say I'd stay."

"Boyo's leaving." Vawn sighed heavily.

"Enjoy the night, dearies. I promise you, this will be your last Christmas."

Caleb scowled at the dark headed woman who barely reached his shoulder. It wasn't until she continued to doomsay to others that he recognized Lachesis— the spinner of fate. She was a nasty Greek goddess he was surprised came to parties at all. "What's up with her?"

Ambrose shrugged. "She's been drinking. Who knows what she'll say."

Aeron arched a brow. "Makes me wonder if she's not telling the truth, then."

"Or," Vawn said, "she's drunk and has no idea what foolishness she's spewing."

Aeron nodded in agreement. "Either way, we should keep her from Acheron lest he tear her apart."

Yeah, they had some serious bitterness in their pasts.

Caleb watched as Lachesis saw Acheron and then dodged through a door, out of his sight. "I guess not everyone is forgiving."

Ambrose let out an evil laugh. "Are you kidding? Acheron isn't the one she should be afraid of. It's Styxx who'll gut her first. I'm surprised she came."

Aeron smiled. "Now *that* would be a happy ending."

Caleb scoffed at the expression he hated almost as much as he hated his parents. "I don't believe in happy endings."

Although, standing in this room, he basically had to eat those words as happy endings were all around him.

How could he deny it?

I'm cursed.

How else could he explain being the odd one out.

It didn't matter. Handing his cup to Aeron, he clapped him on the back. "Merry Christmas. I'm heading home."

Caleb started to teleport out, but decided to walk home. After all, New Orleans was beautiful this time of year. Even if crime was ridiculously high and demons often trolled victims. If he was lucky, one of them might target him.

Now, *that* would be an awesome Christmas present. Beat the crap out of some rando demon who thought he was a tourist ...

The very thought almost brought a smile to his face.

As he wandered, he found himself in front of Bubba Burdette's old store. He smiled at all the memories he had of their misadventures when Ambrose had been in high school and Caleb had first met him.

If only he could go back...

Then again, if he could go back, he wouldn't waste it on Bubba and Mark.

Suddenly, a bright flash behind him brightened the darkness. It reflected off the glass before him where he saw the anguish on his own face.

What now?

Caleb turned, expecting to find an enemy there.

It wasn't an enemy. He staggered back in disbelief at something that couldn't be real.

Was he dreaming?

This wasn't possible.

"Caleb?"

Tears filled his eyes as he came face-to-face with the last person he'd ever thought to see again.

Lil.

His breath caught as the tiny blonde woman approached him hesitantly. Her eyes wide and filled with love, she looked up at him and reached to touch his whiskered cheek.

God, how he wanted to feel her warm hand on his skin. That soothing touch that he'd craved for thousands of centuries.

But this wasn't her. It couldn't be her.

His Lil was gone.

He caught her wrist in his hand to keep her from touching him. "Who are you?"

"It's me, my beautiful demon. I swear."

Her pulse was steady and strong against his palm. "You died. I saw you."

That only seemed to confuse her. "I- I- I... There were demons. An army of them coming for us. I was trying to protect the children. One moment I was ushering them into hiding and the next..." She bit her lip just like she'd always done whenever she was uncertain. "I was in our cave. A man who looked like you, but had different eyes was standing over me. He said that I'd slept enough. That you needed me. I don't understand."

Suspicion raised the hair on the back of his neck. No... she couldn't mean who he thought. "Different eyes, how?"

"One was brown, just like yours. The other was a vivid green."

Jaden.

"My father woke you?"

"Father? He looked more like your brother."

That was his father. "Did he say anything else?"

"He asked me to tell you that he was sorry he couldn't tell you about me. That he didn't dare."

Those words tore through him. His father had kept her all this time? How could he?

Fury reared and he wanted his father's head.

Until Lil touched his cheek.

In that moment, he was taken from the street where they stood to the cave where they'd met.

Where his father waited...

Snarling, Caleb started for him, but Lil caught him against her.

His father's brow bore the weight of sorrow Caleb had felt for all these centuries. "You have every right to hate me. I don't blame you and I know your forgiveness is more than I'll ever deserve. But I couldn't tell you."

"Why not?"

"They would have killed her. Out of spite. Unlike Myone, she's human."

"She was supposed to be immortal!"

Jaden nodded. "That's why she's alive. They didn't know that. I put her in a sleeping trance."

"For eternity?"

Jaden shook his head. "Not quite. I couldn't wake her

while you were enslaved to the Malachais. Have you *any* idea what one of them would have done to her?"

Yes. Actually, he did. And as much as he wanted to gut his father, Caleb knew he was right. They would have taken pleasure in torturing both of them.

And Lil would have ended up dead, anyway.

"Anytime in the last thousand years, you could have told me, you know."

Again, Jaden shook his head. "You needed to be focused, and I didn't think you'd want her to awaken to this world."

There was that. The world had gone to hell. Literally and figuratively.

"So why now?"

Jaden gestured at the two of them. "I can't tell you what the future holds. I lack those powers. But if this is the end, I didn't want you to face it alone. Nor did I want Lilliana to perish in this cave where I hid her." He put their hands together. "You've been apart far too long. Never let anyone or anything divide you again."

Caleb choked on his hate, love, and gratitude. "I hate you, Jaden."

"I know. But never hate her." He stepped back.

The next thing Caleb knew, they were back in New Orleans.

And Lil... *his* Lil... was standing in front of him.

He couldn't believe it. A part of him would never forgive his father for keeping her from him. But it was hard to hate when he finally had the one thing he wanted most.

The one Christmas wish he'd dared not ask because he couldn't stand another bout of disappointment.

Lil was here.

Shaking, and afraid it was all a dream, he picked her up in his arms and kissed her.

This felt too real. She was warm and tasted like happiness.

"Am I really here, Caleb?"

He nodded as tears filled his eyes. "I swear I will spend whatever time we have left proving to you just how much I missed you. And I will never, *ever* let anyone harm you again."

Wrapping her arms around his neck, she smiled. "My precious demon. You will never be alone. I promise."

There was a peculiar note in her voice as she gave him a light kiss. A faint smile played at the edges of her lips. "Do you remember the day you went to battle?"

"It's tortured me for centuries."

"Remember that I told you I had a special gift for when you returned?"

Oddly enough, he'd forgotten that with the horror of everything else that had happened.

"Surely, you don't still have it."

Biting her lip, she wrinkled her nose. "According to your father, I do still have it."

He didn't know what to say to that. How could she have kept a present for all that time.

Unless...

A streak of hope shot through him. He wanted to be wrong and yet he really wanted to be right. "What is it?"

Her smile spread over her face as she whispered in his ear. "We're going to have a baby, my demon. A little Caleb that I hope looks just like his father."

DARK-HUNTER®

Retribution

The Guardian

The Dark-Hunter Companion

Time Untime

Styxx

Dark Bites

Son of No One

Dragonbane

Dragonmark

Dragonsworn

Stygian

Deadmen Walking

Death Doesn't Bargain

At Death's Door

Born of Night

Born of Fire

Born of Ice

Fire & Ice

Born of Shadows

Born of Silence

Cloak & Silence

Born of Fury

Born of Defiance

Born of Betrayal

Born of Legend

Born of Vengeance

Born of Blood

Born of Trouble

Born of Darkness

<u>Lords of Avalon</u>

(written as Kinley MacGregor)

Sword of Darkness

Knight of Darkness

MyKENYON
READ IT. LOVE IT.
www.sherrilynkenyon.com

ABOUT THE AUTHOR

Defying all odds is what #1 New York Times and international bestselling author Sherrilyn Kenyon does best. Rising from extreme poverty as a child that culminated in being a homeless mother with an infant, she has become one of the most popular and influential  authors in the world (in both adult and young adult fiction), with dedicated legions of fans known as Paladins–thousands of whom proudly sport tattoos from her numerous genre-defying series.

Since her first book debuted in 1993 while she was still in college, she has placed more than 80 novels on the New York Times list in all formats and genres, including manga and graphic novels, and has more than 70 million books in print worldwide. Her current series include: Dark-Hunters®, Chronicles of Nick®, Deadman's Cross™, Black Hat Society™, Nevermore™, Silent Swans™, Lords of Avalon® and, The League®.

Over the years, her Lords of Avalon® novels have been adapted by Marvel, and her Dark-Hunters® and Chronicles of Nick® are New York Times bestselling manga and comics and are #1 bestselling adult coloring books.

Join her and her Paladins online at QueenofAll-Shadows.com and www.facebook.com/mysherrilyn.

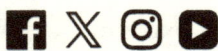

www.ingramcontent.com/pod-product-compliance
Lightning Source LLC
Chambersburg PA
CBHW020154120726
47903CB00007B/2560